CROW BLUE

ADRIANA LISBOA

TRANSLATED FROM PORTUGUESE BY ALISON ENTREKIN

BLOOMSBURY CIRCUS

LONDON · NEW DELHI · NEW YORK · SYDNEY

First published in Great Britain 2013

Work published with the support of Ministry of Culture of Brazil /
National Library Foundation.
Obra publicada com o apoio do Ministério da Cultura do Brasil /
Fundação Biblioteca Nacional.

MINISTÉRIO DA CULTURA
Fundação BIBLIOTECA NACIONAL

Bloomsbury Circus is an imprint of Bloomsbury Publishing Plc
50 Bedford Square
London
WC1B 3DP

www.bloomsbury.com

Bloomsbury Publishing, London, New Delhi, New York and Sydney

A CIP catalogue record for this book is available from the British Library

ISBN 978 1 4088 3830 3
10 9 8 7 6 5 4 3 2 1

Printed and bou...   ...4YY

To Paulo

we are all foreigners
in this city
in this body that awakens

Heitor Ferraz

Periplaneta americana

THE YEAR BEGAN in July. The place was strange. Sweat trickled down inside me, beneath my skin – I sweated and my body stayed dry. It was as if the air was hard, solid, made of stone. I drank glass after glass of water until my belly was bloated and heavy but it was always the same, the dry sweat and the hard air and the sun with a stinger in every ray. There was no breeze, no breath of fresh air slipping through the openings in my blouse, ruffling the hem of my skirt or rustling my hair with the promise of salvation.

On the other hand, I never saw cockroaches.

The American cockroach: *Periplaneta americana*. I once read that they had the ability to regenerate, depending on the severity of the injury. I knew them intimately, personally, as well as by reputation (the only creatures capable of surviving a nuclear holocaust, etc.), from surprise encounters in the kitchen and the hall leading to the service elevator. In Copacabana they were everywhere. But I didn't see any cockroaches in Colorado. It was possible that they were there, and managed to withstand the constant lack of moisture and the harsh winters. But if so they were much more discreet.

I was thirteen. Being thirteen is like being in the middle of nowhere. Which was accentuated by the fact that I was in the middle of nowhere. In a house that wasn't mine, in a city that wasn't mine, in a country that wasn't mine, in a one-man family that, in spite of the intersections and intentions (all very good), wasn't mine.

My knuckles turned white, threatening to split. It was weird. I seemed to be progressively transforming into something else, as if undergoing a slow mutation.

Maybe I was becoming a lizard or one of those plants that can flourish in the desert. Maybe I was mineralizing and turning into a river, the temporary sort that vanishes into the parched riverbed in the dry season, and then swells and tumbles happily along as if that's all there is to it, tumbling happily along, peril-free. As if its own life as a river wasn't seasonal and brittle.

More than once I thought, in the first few months, that it wasn't a place made for humans, any more than it was for cockroaches. And yet humans had lived there for thirteen millennia, arm-wrestling with the place, long before the gold and silver mines of the nineteenth century. Long before Buffalo Bill.

In that month of July, the first month of my New Year, Fernando took me to a public swimming pool. Fair-skinned people sprawled in deck chairs in pursuit of a tan that was long in the coming, and which, when it arrived, had a reddish tinge that was too obvious, too red.

Like the other Latinos, and people from India, my already very brown skin became even browner after an hour of sun. I didn't really know what to do with all that easy, impulsive melanin, which willingly gave itself up to the sun as if it were a volunteer in some sacrificial rite.

A woman passing my chair as she returned from the pool said I had a nice tan. When she smiled, her eyes disappeared into the folds of fat that covered her face. She looks like a feather pillow, I thought. She was wearing a skirted bathing suit and had very small hands at the end of doughy arms, and she walked as if she was afraid to touch the ground with her chubby feet. She walked as if the ground hurt.

Elegance? I wondered. No, not elegance. Perhaps a certain mistrust of the act of walking. Perhaps she was trying to remind us that we need to be ceremonious with the world, that this here is no joke, that this is something serious and dangerous, and that the mere act of walking on the ground bestows an unimaginable responsibility on you. Or maybe it was just the way she walked and had nothing to do with responsibility, nor was it, come to think of it, anyone else's business.

In the swimming pool, I surfaced next to a good-looking man with thick cords of muscle wrapped around his firm arms. When I looked at him close up I noticed that he had blond eyelashes. I didn't know there were people with blond eyelashes. The good-looking man was exchanging smiles and words (more smiles than words) with a flexible young woman with flawless eyebrows.

I sank under again and opened my eyes underwater and saw a multitude of legs of various shapes, sizes, colors and thicknesses

– the tentacles of a chlorinated-water Leviathan, waving back and forth in a disorderly, unsynchronized fashion.

Before, in Copacabana, there were: miniscule bikinis. Butt-cheeks hanging out. A few women here and there rubbing perox-ide on their legs to bleach their hairs. Depending on the place, lots of children. Depending on the place, a few prostitutes. Muscular bodies jogging in the sun. Flaccid bodies jogging in the sun. Tight Speedos outlining men's balls and revealing what side their penises were on. When I had nothing else to do, on the beach, I used to run a tally, to see if more men kept their penises on the left side or on the right.

Now, in Lakewood, there were: large bikinis and full-piece bathing suits in fabrics that sometimes bunched up around the backside. Men in board-shorts. At the edge of the pool, people eating hamburgers and French fries and drinking beer and soft drinks in king-size paper cups.

The size of things surprised me.

Are they very expensive? I asked Fernando.

No, he said. Do you want one?

I said no. And I thanked him, as my mother had taught me to do.

The year began in July. Not exactly when the immigration official checked my American passport (which identified me, but with which I still didn't identify). The year had begun a few weeks earlier, when Fernando called.

I had already packed my only suitcase when he called. I had put everything important into it, but when I went to organize it I discovered that 'important' is a flimsy category. It doesn't stand up on its own. The memory of an onion after it has been peeled. The idea you have of the onion that doesn't necessarily correspond to the actual onion. The tears caused by the onion, which originate at the very end of a whole complex chain of enzymes, gases, nerve endings and glands, as Mrs. Mojo explained at some stage in school (on the same day, incidentally, that Mrs. Mitchell revealed that pizza had been invented in Chicago).

Almost everything 'important' wasn't when confronted with brave, staring-contest eyes.

I considered my things:

Those books I had already read: I wasn't going to reread them, was I? Did it make any sense to lug around a collection of paper paving-stones with colorful covers as if they were pets: half-blind, slobbery dogs needing extra care at the end of their lives?

Those two pairs of sneakers: one hurt my heel. It was the nicer-looking one but it hurt my heel. The confrontation between beauty and utility can sometimes be uncomfortable, and the utility of an uncomfortable pair of sneakers somewhat obscure and uncertain. Besides, there would always be someone in the world with feet a little different to mine – more delicate, without such a prominent bone in the corner. That person would be Cinderella to my nicer-looking pair of sneakers, and it was up to me to bid them farewell and hope that they lived happily ever after.

Those four pairs of earrings of which I only really liked three but only really wore two and I wouldn't even need two, since I only have one pair of ears: it was better to donate three of the four pairs to someone more appearance-conscious, with less migratory plans than mine. Not least because the fewer earrings one has, the fewer one loses. If I kept that one pair of earrings in day and night, there was a good chance they'd be with me for a long time, and luckily ears weren't feet and earrings weren't shoes.

Plush toys? Silly, useless collectors of dust mites. I could donate them to a silly, useless child and the dust mites would be well deserved.

And so on.

My warm-weather clothes, ninety percent of my wardrobe, would only be useful part of the year. My cold-weather clothes wouldn't stand up to the cold: a sweatshirt for freezing-cold temperatures?

But what exactly were freezing-cold temperatures? I opened Elisa's freezer, closed my eyes and inhaled a frost-free world, trying to imagine it. Minus five? Wind chill factor of minus twenty? Was it true that your nose and ears could freeze and fall off? Your fingertips? (I recently discovered in the magazine *Men's Talk* that there are worse things and that the people who climb Mount Everest have to face minus ninety degrees Fahrenheit. I learned this in a column written by a man who defined himself as an *orthodox Flamengo supporter, who plays the drums, loves beer and women – in that order – and is a doctor in his spare time.* In other sections of the magazine were articles such as: *Mystery solved: why women always go to restrooms in pairs. Tips for pairing food and wine on New Year's Eve. How to invest in real estate faster than you think possible.*)

How many closed shoes do you have? Elisa asked.

Two, these two pairs of sneakers, but one hurts me.

Elisa sighed. What size are you?

Six.

She went into her room and came back with a pair of imitation-leather shoes with low heels.

Take these, they're a seven but they'll fit. If you have an important occasion and can't wear sneakers.

I couldn't imagine what important occasion I might have. Fernando worked as a security guard at a public library. In his spare time he made a bit of extra cash as a cleaner. He wasn't married and he didn't have any kids. I doubted that important occasions were a part of his everyday life. But Elisa, my mother's foster sister, wanted me to take the pair of heels anyway.

You never know, she said.

One year ended in July and another began in July, but they weren't connected to one another. There were twelve months between the two that weren't on the calendar. Kind of like those ten days Pope Gregory XIII yanked out of the month of October in order to institute the calendar that we have all come to follow – we being, at least: me, Elisa, my mother when she was alive, and the immigration official at Atlanta Airport and the woman in the skirted bathing suit at the public swimming pool in Lakewood, and also the man with blond eyelashes and his slender consort and their smiles full of sexual innuendos and their knees touching under the water. I had studied Gregory XIII and his calendar at school; part of that onslaught of what seemed like random information that they shoveled on to us during long hours that turned into weeks that turned into months that turned into the next school year. I don't know what the pope did with those ten stolen days. Maybe they are in the same non-place as the twelve months in which I lived with Elisa, crowned by that packing of suitcases, or rather, suitcase, and the stripping away of all excesses. At some stage close to the end of those twelve months, I packed my suitcase with the important things, which had already shrunk to the barest minimum, and waited for Fernando's phone call.

I never did use the shoes that Elisa gave me. To be honest, I didn't like them, the gold buckles in the corner. Besides which, they really were too big for me: there was a one-centimeter gap between my heels and the backs of the shoes if my big toes were touching the front of them. When I walked, the heels would slap up with a brief delay, like flip-flops.

I really didn't care for heels anyway. I didn't at the age of thirteen, and I still don't at twenty-two. Elisa's shoes are still untouched in my wardrobe to this day. I don't like high heels. What's more, at twenty-two I still wear a size six.

Lakewood, Colorado. A strange place. But its strangeness didn't bother me, because that Denver suburb was, to me, a mere stepping-stone. Something I was using to achieve an objective. A bridge, a ritual, a password that you utter before a door and wait for someone to open it, while you tap your feet on the sidewalk, looking around for the sake of it. Being there was being in transit, and Lakewood and I had no relevance in each other's lives.

Alone at home, those first few afternoons, I looked out the window and saw the immensity of the sky nudged by the mountains in the west. There was some green, but it was so paltry that, for me, it didn't count. As far as I was concerned, green was either exuberant and dense or it wasn't green. I didn't consider those stunted little desert plants green. The trees on the street seemed useless, an unsuccessful attempt to prove something unprovable; the air swallowed them, the space swallowed them.

Before, I was accustomed to walking along under trees. I moved along Copacabana's dirty, narrow streets and bulging sidewalks with a canopy of leaves overhead all year round. Now, I found myself in a semiarid city where the streets were wide and clean and there was no shade to be found.

Before, it was exaggerated tropicality, with relative humidity somewhere in the vicinity of eighty percent. Perfect for cockroaches. The cockroaches were so happy in Rio de Janeiro, that easy, welcoming place. Now, the relative humidity was about thirty percent.

And there was the waterless, sterile heat, which left my body dry and my skin like a sheet of paper. Use lots of moisturizer, a woman on the plane told me. I rubbed in moisturizer three or four times a day. All over my body, face and lips. At night it hurt to breathe.

You get used to it, said Fernando.

That was something Fernando knew a lot about. Getting used to things. After a time I would look at him and see the man-who-got-used-to-things.

He could work as a farm laborer in São João do Araguaia, he could survive behind the bar of a London pub and in the dry air of Lakewood, Colorado. He could survive entire armies and half-lived love affairs. Women who disappeared. Women for whom he needed to disappear. Crossing borders and ideologies. He could even survive me and my sudden reappearance, popping out of a box like one of those clowns with a spring for a neck. And he could say OK, as he had done. There was something heroic about it.

I soon noticed that the dryness of the air had some advantages. For example, I could leave my bath towel bunched up any old which way after a shower, and what in Rio de Janeiro would have remained tenaciously in the folds, evolving into a stench and finally mold, in that lascivious commitment to life, that embarrassing explosion of fecundity and virility of the tropics, in Colorado quickly rose up to the heavens and was no more, and the towel would sit there, dry and stiff, a makeshift statue.

In Copacabana, Rio de Janeiro, there were cockroaches, almond trees, mosquitoes, salty air, pigeons. Churches. Mundial Supermarket. McDonald's. In Lakewood, Colorado, there were rabbits, prairie dogs, crows. Churches. SuperTarget. McDonald's.

I decided to be absolutely, unflinchingly courageous. Whatever my life was, happy or unhappy or none of the above, it was my business. Besides which, these categories seemed as untrustworthy as 'important' had been when I was packing my suitcase. I was going to do whatever had to be done and it wasn't going to be my dry nose at night that was going to make me feel sorry for myself, after everything that had happened. No way. My situation was osseous; it was of the order of structures, without flesh, without glaze. I fit in a thirteen-year-old body and all of my material belongings now fit in a suitcase weighing twenty kilos. And everything was guided by the potential shadow of the past — a midday shadow, that you don't see, but which knows how to conceal itself in things, ready to start leaking out across the ground as soon as the planet turns a little to one side.

In general, I didn't do much in those first few days in Colorado. I stared out the window at the street, and the street stared back at me, disinterested. We both yawned. I avoided looking at myself in the mirror. I got shocks when I touched door handles because of the static electricity. I tidied what could be tidied in the house, and considered it a way of paying Fernando back, albeit insufficiently, for taking me in, like when Elisa had put me up.

I was given instructions on how to use the washing machine, the dryer, the dishwasher, the microwave and the electric oven (you have to be VERY careful when using the electric oven, Fernando said three times, and mentally I said for fuck's sake, Fernando, I'm not deaf or dumb).

A pair of used skates appeared from somewhere, and when there was the slightest scrap of a cloud in the sky, making the sun a little less vehement, I went skating around the neighborhood. A block further each day. Expanding my circle of influence. Marking my territory in a territory that wasn't mine, as a well-meaning but mistaken animal would, using his bodily fluids. Doing it for the sake of it. And the trees were always few, always short and frail, even when they weren't, because the wide streets and the empty spaces and the sky, like arrogant gods, compelled them, with a raised index finger, to wither.

It was the first time in my life I'd noticed the relative size of things. Everything was small in that place. Even when Fernando took me to see Denver's rich southern suburbs. The enormous two- and three-story houses were painted neutral colors and sat there as placid and sleepy as cakes displayed on the counter of a giant confectioner's store. After a while it all began to seem a bit danger-ous, like a recurrent nightmare in which nothing actually happened but there was a promise of something macabre in the stillness of the air, in the absence of people walking down the street, in the conformity of the lawns that were like fake smiles, in the tame, ball-shaped bushes: circus performers.

A man in a gaudy T-shirt rode past us on a bicycle. His thigh muscles rippled under the tight fabric of his black shorts which were padded in the backside. He was wearing a pointy helmet with a rear-view mirror. I had never seen a helmet with a rear-view mirror.

It was strange not to see people walking down the street. I thought of a post-apocalyptic world in which the air was unhealthy and the people had to protect themselves, zipping back and forth between the insides of their houses and the insides of their cars and the insides of commercial establishments.

I found it strange that the stores, all gigantic, had *their backs* to the sidewalks (maybe that was why no one was walking around) and opened their doors onto bulging parking lots with marked parking spaces and oceans of SUVs.

I tried to calculate the number of rooms in the houses by the number of windows – they must have had six, seven, eight rooms.

But, even there, what was in excess was the sky stretching over-head and the flat ground that ran into the alpine dissidence of the Rocky Mountains in the west, rising up over fourteen thousand feet, and extended monotonously in every other direction for what was left of the state as far as Nebraska, Kansas and Oklahoma in the east, New Mexico in the south and Wyoming in the north. Those new names whose history and meaning I tried to dig out of the collective unconscious.

Flat, smooth, dry, tedious, dusty, uniform, continuous, constant, boring, unattractive: this was my impression of the plains in the first few months. What existed there was the dictatorship of space: an infinity of ground to the right, an infinity of mountains to the left, an infinity of sky cloaking everything.

The mansions of Denver's wealthy suburbs couldn't be considered anything but ridiculous in their ambition to compete with the space. The seven rooms, or however many there were, ten, twenty, were nothing. Up high, on their western trail, the mountains were laughing their heads off at it all. The mountains were even laughing their heads off at the buildings in downtown Denver. When you arrived at the International Airport, the city centre was a tiny cluster the size of a marble. In it you could barely make out the skyscrapers, which didn't scrape the sky at all, because the Colorado sky had yet to be scraped by human hands of concrete: the fifty-six floors of the Republic Plaza, the fifty-two of the Qwest tower (where you read, at the top: Qwest), the fifty of the cash-register-shaped building. None of it made the slightest difference. Not the mansions, or the buildings, or the artificially green golf courses in the middle of the almost-desert aridity. Reality obeyed another scale.

Maybe that was why I had the feeling, right from the very first day, that the sky was lower there – and, even so, far above the skyscrapers, both present and future. As soon as I left the well-behaved density of downtown Denver, along came that enormous solitude to crush everything in existence: flesh, metal, leaf, trunk, stone. A solitude imposed by the space. A solitude of disperse atoms, of things out of stock on supermarket shelves.

You lose a little self-certainty when confronted with this. And when I went off exploring Fernando's neighborhood in those first few weeks, on skates, I found the small houses humbler and more appropriate, as if they were bowing their heads, and there the people who smiled and greeted me seemed to share a little of that same solitude. As if their smiles said: tell me about it.

In those days, avid for information, I read that the entire state of Colorado had fewer inhabitants than the city of Rio de Janeiro. And I knew that the mountains of Rio de Janeiro, albeit for other reasons, were also laughing at their city. Those tropical mountains that had been stripped of entire forests. Mountains that had risen up out of the ground by the sea, which the city scaled and scaled, on which people built as best they could with whatever materials were to hand. The constructions subsided from time to time with the rains and people rebuilt them as best they could.

The mountains didn't discriminate. The relationship was different there: the city grew on top of them, rolling boulders. It reminded me of a story my mother had once told me about the unfortunate Greek King Sisyphus, who, because of a mess he'd gotten himself into (the mythological Greeks were always getting into trouble: they were megalomaniacs and undisciplined), was sentenced by the gods to roll an enormous boulder up a steep hill. But it kept rolling back down and he had to start all over again. I imagined those sadistic Greek gods watching Sisyphus work for all of eternity like a group of old ladies sitting around drinking tea, reeking of sweet perfume and making comments dripping with avarice and bitter frustration about the sinful ways of the new generations. With pieces of cake stuck to their teeth and eyebrows that had been plucked too thin.

From the mountains of Rio de Janeiro people: went hang-gliding. Fired guns. Saw the rest of Rio de Janeiro down below and the crashing waves that looked like a motionless strip of white foam.

The mountains of Rio de Janeiro were laughing, deep in their intimacy of earth and stone and roots and organic matter from dead leaves and animals and dumped dead bodies; they were laughing at all that anxious human drama: people love one another, kill one another, roll boulders, and at the end of the day none of it makes much difference. The mountains' time is different; so are their frames of reference.

Maybe it had all begun thirteen millennia earlier. Or thirteen years. How could I be sure? Perhaps by prodding the wound that wasn't exactly a wound (and anyway everyone had more serious things to worry about). Perhaps by talking to the ghost of William F. Cody, the original Buffalo Bill (people visiting his grave could *feel the breezes from the high peaks of the Continental Divide, smell the pines and watch the mountain wildlife, all just thirty minutes from downtown Denver.* See something? Hear something?) Perhaps by reading the message in a handful of magic sand at the Chimayo sanctuary, while the woman cried *me puedes ayudar, un dólar por favor* (it was her job, like the guy who used to take his shirt off, dislocate his shoulder and beg for money in the middle of downtown Rio de Janeiro: people would grimace involuntarily when they saw him and give him some loose change. Then the man would go behind the Municipal Theater and put his shoulder back in place). I would give the woman the dollar she was asking for while Fernando ignored her, asking in a low voice how I could fall for it, but it was my money and my problem.

The world didn't owe me anything, but it didn't stop me from haphazardly following a haphazardly-drawn path, which was of no importance in anyone's life, and which could have passed as in fact it did: on the sidelines of everything. Almost a blank.

But let's just say, for the sake of this story, that everything began with her. Thirteen years earlier.

Crotalus atrox

SHE WAS THE one who had taught me English and Spanish. It was what she knew how to do. If she'd been a yoga teacher, she'd have spent twelve years teaching me yoga, and if she'd worked on the land I'd have had a hoe before I'd even learned to talk. It was what she knew how to do, and she thought it a waste not to pass on to me, for free, as an inheritance, some kind of knowledge.

It was English and Spanish because she'd lived in the United States, in Texas and New Mexico, for twenty-two years, and if there's one thing that twenty-two years in a place will impose on you it is mastery of the local language, even if you don't have any special talent for it.

My mother had learned English formally at school. Spanish, informally, with the *tejanos*.

And I learned both from my mother, submitting to her lessons with a resistance that was never any match for hers.

¿Es el televisor?

No, senõr (señorita, señora), no es el televisor. Es el gato.
Once upon a time there were four little Rabbits, and their names
were —

  Flopsy,

    Mopsy,

      Cottontail,

        and Peter.

(Later on I saw Peter Rabbit in supermarkets at Easter. I remembered my mother. I also remembered Flopsy, Mopsy and Cottontail, who were very good little rabbits and thus escaped life's punishments, though they lacked Peter's heroic charm.)

The mothers in my family die young. By the age of nine my mother had lost her mother and gone to Texas with her geologist father. A work opportunity for him, which he'd gotten through his contacts' contacts' contacts.

My mother grew up in Texas. One day (she never told me why, and somehow I didn't think I should ask) she severed ties with her father and moved to New Mexico.

My mother liked severing ties with men and disappearing from their lives. The tendency began there, with my geologist grandfather.

She found a little house in Albuquerque, near Route 66, with its old-fashioned charm, more than a decade before I was born. One of those little adobe houses, with a flat roof resting on wooden beams that ran horizontally through the walls.

She still lived in this house when I was born. We lived there until I was two. I visited it much later, with Fernando and Carlos, my improbable pair of travel companions, one icy November day.

It was a small house of the most absolute simplicity, as if it had sprung from the ground itself.

My mother made her living teaching English to Mexicans migrating back to New Mexico – some time after the Americans had migrated there, as she liked to say. Who was foreign there, who was a local? What language did the land speak? (In essence, it didn't speak English or Spanish, because the people who were there when the explorers and conquistadores arrived were Navajo and Anasazi and Ute. And others. And others before them. But none with the surnames Coronado or Oñate, no one known as Cabeza de Vaca. Or Billy the Kid.)

My mother also taught Spanish to Americans. University students sometimes sought her out. Some, very few, wanted to learn Portuguese. By this time it was the least fluent of her three languages. But because of her students she delved into Brazilian music and films and books. The few Americans interested in Brazil made my mother rediscover Brazil, perhaps a little clumsily at first, with the awkwardness of the prodigal child who returns home with their hands in their pockets and drooping ears. But who a short time later are crossing their feet on the table and flicking cigarette butts into corners.

I don't remember my early childhood in Albuquerque, of course. When I travel back in time, it feels as though I was born in Rio de Janeiro. More specifically, on Copacabana Beach – right there on the sand, among the pigeons and the litter left behind by beach-goers. I think of Copacabana. I close my eyes and even if I'm listening to *Acoustic Arabia* and burning Japanese Zen-Buddhist temple incense, what reaches my senses is a faint whiff of sea breeze, a faint taste of fruit popsicles mixed with sand and salt water. And the sound of the waves fizzing on the sand, and the popsicle vendor's voice under the moist Rio sun.

I remember the light, my fingers digging tunnels and building castles in the wet sand, patiently. There were other children around, but we were all the beginning, middle and end of our own private universes. We played together, that is, sharing space in a kind of tense harmony, but it was as if each child were cocooned in his or her own bubble of ideas, sensations, initiatives, and state-of-the-art architectural projects involving wet sand and popsicle sticks.

So I was born at the age of two on Copacabana Beach, and it was always summer, but a summer wedded to water, and my tools for changing the world – for altering it and shaping it and making it worthy of me – were a little red bucket and a yellow sieve, spade and rake.

And further along was a horizon to which I gave no thought. The imaginary line where the sky and sea parted company, liquid to one side, not liquid to the other. A kind of concrete abstract.

I left the horizon in peace and preferred to dream of islands, which were real, and which maybe I'd be able to swim to if I ever got serious about swimming, and which were separated by a world of different shadows, a world where speeds and sounds were different, where animals very different to me lived. A world of fish, of algae, of mollusks, of crow-blue shells – like those I would read about in a poem, much later. A whole other life, another register, but a human being could actually swim between them, observe them, dive to the ocean floor in Copacabana and touch the intimacy of the sand, there, so far from the popsicle sticks and volleyballs and *empada* vendors. The intimacy that was completely alien to the usual chaos of the neighborhood of Copacabana, where people hurried along or dawdled with the elderly gait of the retired or mugged or got mugged or queued at the bank or lifted weights at the gym or begged at traffic lights or pretended not to see people begging at traffic lights or looked at the pretty woman or were the pretty woman with the tiny triangles of her bikini top or tallied up prices on the supermarket cash register or picked up litter from the sidewalks and streets or tossed litter on the sidewalks and streets or sold sex to tourists or wrote poems or walked their dogs. The drama of the city didn't even figure in the subconscious of the ocean floor. It wasn't important or relevant. It didn't even exist there.

The horizon was the theme of those who yearned for the impossible. So they could keep on yearning, I guess. I've always thought it was complacent to search for something you're never going to find. Pondering the poetry and symbolism of the horizon wasn't for me. I preferred to ponder islands and fish.

Or, better yet, the architecture of the castle I was building that morning, which was not going to crumble this time. I was making some improvements to the project, which had already failed several times.

There were children and adults around me; I was aware of their existence more or less peripherally. We could get along well if we didn't bother one another, if we interacted as little as possible. The beach was large and free of charge, the sun was for everyone.

★ ★ ★

In Rio, my mother also taught English and Spanish. And Portuguese to foreigners. She said it was a Wild-Card Profession and she said it like she meant it. Anywhere in the world, there would always be people wanting to learn English and/or Spanish. And Portuguese – Portuguese would increase its sphere of influence after Brazil showed the world what it was made of.

You'll live to see it, she'd say, straightening her back and lifting her chin as she spoke, as if defying the very air in front of her to contradict her.

When we went to live in Brazil, she became a nationalist. An advocate of all things Brazilian, among them the language we had inherited from our European colonizer and acclimatized, and which she came to consider the most beautiful in the world.

It was the 1990s and she *voted in the presidential elections*. All Brazilians of age *voted in the presidential elections*. They were still getting used to this degree of democracy, but they'd get there one day, she'd say. We'll get there. If I hadn't been such a small child at the time, I might have asked how, if the first thing that the first democratically elected president in three decades had done, on his first day in office, was to confiscate the money in people's savings accounts. He promised it would be returned at a later date. This happened a year before we returned to Brazil and my mother hadn't felt the brunt of it, but Elisa no doubt ranted and raved and uttered swear words that I could have memorized for future reference if I'd been present and able to understand her. But, at the end of the day, they were adults and should have known what they were doing, electing, confiscating, swearing.

My mother and I never returned to Albuquerque together. In fact, we never returned to the United States together.

Firstly, because she no longer got paid in US dollars for her lessons, and in Brazil human resources were pretty cheap, even perfectly trilingual human resources, so the trip was too expensive for our new green and yellow more-or-less-underpaid pockets.

Secondly, because my mother wasn't one to retrace her steps. When she left, she left. When she walked out, she walked out.

In the long summer holidays, we always went to Barra do Jucu, in the state of Espírito Santo, where my mother had friends. We'd climb into her Fiat 147 and some seven hours later we'd arrive, weary and happy, and along the way my mother would listen to music and sing along, and we'd stop at diners that smelled of grease and burnt coffee to use restrooms that smelled of urine and disinfectant, where a very fat employee sat crocheting and sold crocheted doilies and underwear next to a cardboard box that said TIPS PLEASE.

My mother would play Janis Joplin and turn up the volume and stick her head out the window of her Fiat 147 and sing along, as if she was in a film:

Freedom's just another word for nothing left to lose,
Nothing don't mean nothing honey if it ain't free, now now.

Even when I didn't understand the words, I was hypnotized by my mother's trance. She seemed like another woman, which fascinated and frightened me. Her voice had a hoarseness exactly like Janis Joplin's and I wondered why some people became Janis Joplin and others became my mother.

You sing just as well as Janis Joplin, I once told her.

The only thing we have in common is that her dad worked for Texaco, she replied. You know. Oil.

When I was informed that Janis Joplin had died in 1970, almost two decades before I was born, I was indignant. I had thought Janis Joplin was my contemporary, and that she was singing "Me & Bobby McGee" somewhere on the planet, while my mother, who was everything Janis Joplin hadn't been, who was her opposite, her antimatter in another dimension, was sticking her head out the window of the car that wasn't a Porsche painted in psychedelic colors and belting out what she could to the scalding-hot asphalt of the highway.

In Barra do Jucu, my mother sometimes went out dancing at night, or to meet someone for a few beers.

Two of these someones became boyfriends who lasted a few summers. One of them came to visit us in Rio. The other one lived in Rio, was a surfer and had a five-year-old boy whom I envied, secretly and angrily. In Rio and Barra do Jucu, my mother's boyfriend started teaching me to surf, but then things between them ground to a halt. He called me for a few months to ask how things were going and to try to discover, between the lines, if my mother had met someone else, and if this someone else seemed more likable than him, and why. I became the surfer's ally, but it was no good. One day he stopped calling, and I stopped surfing.

My mother's friends in Barra do Jucu also had young kids. We liked to watch the crabs in the mangrove swamp right behind the house – the crabs held a terrible fascination for me and, though horrified and disgusted, I couldn't keep my eyes off their slow, muddy walk, those lone monks in their long meditative trances.

The other kids and I changed from pajamas into beachwear and from beachwear into pajamas, after a hose-down at the end of each day. Someone always butted in with a bar of soap and a bottle of shampoo: growing up is a drag. But I was violently happy there, and returned from Barra do Jucu when the holidays were over with skin the color of dark wood, almost like the jacaranda table in our living room.

Elisa used to call me her little caramel girl. Elisa was my mother's foster sister.

My family's genealogy is confusing and simple at the same time. My grandmother brought up Elisa as if she were her own daughter. Later my mother was born and then my grandmother died, and when my mother went to Texas with my grandfather, Elisa stayed in Rio. She was all grown up, sixteen years old, and had a job and a fiancé who would never become her husband but was a fiancé nonetheless, which was better than nothing. Unlike his real daughter, she never severed ties with the man who had brought her up, though she never saw him again either, because there was an entire continent between them, and when my retired-geologist Brazilian grandfather died of a Texan snakebite on Texan soil at the age of sixty-seven, she was the one who broke the news to my mother, all the way from the southern hemisphere.

Elisa was the daughter who had accidentally sprung from the womb of my mother's mother's maid. There was no father in the picture. The mother died in childbirth.

I'll bring her up, said my grandmother, and that was how Elisa came into the family.

But she'd always be the maid's daughter, and this original sin, this hybridism with the dark world of the servant class, in a caste system deeply rooted in Brazilian society from day one, set her apart from my mother, who went to the United States, while Elisa stayed behind after my grandmother's death. If she nursed any hurt feelings like tiny secret jewels at the bottom of a drawer, she never let on to me. Later she studied to be a nurse and got a job in the public service and broke off her engagement because her fiancé kept stalling. According to Elisa, it was better to be alone than in a dead-end relationship.

As for me, when someone asked me what I wanted to be when I grew up the only things that occurred to me were occupations that took place on a strip of sand with waves breaking against it. *Empada* vendor? Thus, the years spent in Copacabana and Barra do Jucu, with the powerful machine known as the Fiat 147, suited me one hundred percent. And except for a living Janis Joplin, I wanted for nothing, ever.

But there were still the Spanish and English lessons. This way you'll get work anywhere in the world, my mother used to say.

And I'd mentally recite:

¿Es el televisor?

No, señor (señorita, señora), no es el televisor. Es el gato.

I didn't want to work anywhere in the world explaining to people that cats weren't TVs. But putting up resistance to the transmission/imposition of knowledge was pointless.

My mother told me stories about her mother. About her father she only said the barest minimum.

I imagined my grandmother as a very thin woman with tiny feet who collected postcards from places with suggestive names like Hanover and Islamabad. She had a cat that lay in her lap and bit everyone else. An eccentric cat, who preferred his teeth to his claws. One day the cat fell out the apartment window and died, splayed across the sidewalk. People said the cat had committed suicide.

My mother told me that she'd told them that cats don't commit suicide.

How do you know? I asked her.

Cats don't commit suicide, she repeated.

I imagined my grandfather in a cowboy hat, selling his geological knowledge to oil companies in Texas. And one day getting bitten by a lethal rattlesnake called *Crotalus atrox*. He had a blue suit jacket and a roll of fat at the nape of his neck.

My grandparents had names. My grandmother was Maria Gorete, a name I've never seen on anyone else. There must be other Maria Goretes in the world. But for me 'Maria Gorete' is synonymous with 'grandmother', and a specific grandmother. My grandfather, her husband, was Abner, which was something biblical, with the usual biblical grandiosity.

Maria Gorete and Abner were Elisa's foster parents and my mother Suzana's parents for real. They were my grandparents for real, even though I never met them. And not the grandparents of the children that Elisa never had.

This was my family tree until I was thirteen years old. One man and four women across three generations. Odd arithmetic, tied up like colorful handkerchiefs inside a magician's top hat. A family tree lacking roots, which in the place of certain branches only had vague gestures, indications, suggestions, forget-about-its.

27

If you look at it from another point of view, however, things were very simple.

After all, sometimes people vanish.

But sometimes other people go looking for them. They pull their colorful handkerchiefs out of their top hats, dragging out rabbits, doves and even a burning torch, to the audience's astonishment.

Maria Gorete, my grandmother, liked to play with dolls even as an adult. She liked to sing a song about a lamb, which never failed to make my mother cry. *I used to have a little lamb, Jasmine was her name. Her wool was fleecy white, and when I called she came.* When she had visitors over and wanted to show off her daughter, Maria Gorete would say: Do you want to see her cry? And she'd sing. *A hunter in the flowering fields* (my mother's eyes would already be brimming over) *shot her down one day.* And Maria Gorete would recite: *When I got to her she was dead, and I cried in dismay.*

And my mother would cry.

How cute, visitor no. 1 would say.

She's so sensitive, visitor no. 2 would say.

No, she's just silly, Maria Gorete would say.

My mother would tell me this story and I secretly agreed with Maria Gorete: how silly to cry over a lamb in a song. But my mother always cried again when she sang the song to me and I knew that she wasn't asking my opinion and that it was better not to say anything. Besides which, I also thought it was silly of Maria Gorete to play with dolls as an adult. And I thought it was the height of silliness for Maria Gorete to show off her daughter to visitors by making her cry, and over such an unworthy thing. I decided they deserved each other.

Maria Gorete fell ill and died. Two years before Janis Joplin. My mother inherited her dolls, and later, when she was living in the United States and thought she was too big to play with dolls, she donated them all to a Presbyterian orphanage in Dallas. All but one, Priscila, which she kept and, when I was deemed big enough, gave to me as a present. Which was a mistake. I wasn't big enough and did Priscila's makeup with a pen. Washing her was useless. She was left with a smudged, end-of-party look for the rest of time.

The day I arrived from Brazil, I hung the clothes I had in the closet. There weren't many. In the front entrance of Fernando's house in Lakewood, Colorado, there was a closet for coats and shoes. I put Elisa's heels, which I was never going to use, in it. The heels half-closed their eyes and there they stayed, like a Hindu ascetic going to meditate in a cave.

When you come inside, take your shoes off, Fernando told me. That way the house stays clean for longer.

Then he went to his room and came back with a bag.

Here, Evangelina, I bought these for you. They're to wear around the house.

In the bag was a pair of checkered slippers that were fleecy on the inside. I thought they looked like granny slippers, but I didn't say anything.

They're not for now, of course, he said. They're for when it gets cold.

You can call me Vanja, I said.

Fernando's house had two bedrooms. He got the sofa bed ready for me in the spare bedroom. Later on we'll have to buy you a coat and some boots, he said. There's a shop with some good stuff at the outlet. But it doesn't have to be right away.

It didn't have to be ever. It was unimaginable that at some point I was going to feel cold there. Boots? He had to be kidding.

But contrary to all of my expectations and everything that pointed to a new world one hundred percent untouched in its desert rigidity, it started to rain every now and again.

The first rain fell during the night. I woke up and everything was wet, but it didn't last. The sun re-confiscated all of the water on the ground, on the heroic plants. And it was as if nothing had happened. It was as if someone had committed a faux pas at dinner and everyone present had forgotten it in a hurry.

The second was in the afternoon, a fine rain, and I had the impression that it gave up and evaporated halfway between the clouds and the earth. A weird rain, that didn't wet the ground.

The third was a storm that lasted nineteen minutes, accompanied by lightening and thunder. I observed the miracle from the window, fascinated.

It's raining quite a bit this summer, said Fernando. One Saturday, when everything was dry again, he got his red 1985 Saab and took me down Highway 93, hugging the mountains, to the city of Boulder. Along the way I saw a drag racing track. In Boulder, he bought two tire tubes and blew them up at a gas station and we rode down a section of the river with our backsides in the holes, hollering and overturning on the rocks and grazing our knees.

Then I sat in the shade by the river's edge and watched skaters, uniformed cyclists, Labradors and a bum with dreadlocks go past.

One day I went to my future school on roller skates and for the first time I felt real fear, the sort that can send shivers through you even when outside waves of heat are lifting up off the asphalt like something supernatural. It was the hottest time of day and the public school was closed for the holidays, and its muteness evoked something secret and dangerous. Maybe military research was carried out or political prisoners were arbitrarily held in there.

One morning, a month from then, I walked through those doors together with new and old students. I was still in my early teens, but I already suspected that adolescence was basically a declared war between me and adulthood.

Later I discovered it wasn't really like that; more the simple, mundane fact that my ideas were suddenly clear in my mind, and in my mind only, while everyone else made one mistake after another.

Everyone else wore the wrong clothes, listened to the wrong music and said the wrong things at the wrong time, read the wrong books, drove the wrong way, sniffled and used toothpicks, had family lunches on Sundays, got married, got divorced, died, was born, and check out the moustache on that man, and check out that woman in those awful soccer-players' shorts.

My messianic wave came and went, for lack of disciples, or the wrong marketing strategy. It was destined to be brief. But before I realized that I personified a secular combination of Jesus, Buddha, Muhammad and Deepak Chopra, and then succumbed to the weight of responsibility and gave it all up, Fernando had already let me know what he thought about school and its dangers.

Careful about this thing of being popular, he said. Run from the word. Popular. Also run from the word loser. Don't say these things. Don't think them. Don't divide the world into popular and unpopular people, winners and losers. All that crap.

Then he apologized for saying crap.

After three weeks of school Aditi Ramagiri and I were already saying how Jake Moore was a loser. A big time loser. A mega-loser. Such a complete and utter loser that there was no possible salvation for him. It wasn't even worth growing up and becoming an adult. He'd be a loser as an adult too. I don't remember exactly why, but I remember that when Jake Moore went past, Aditi and I would look at one another and whisper: loser.

I found out on my own, a little later, that the opposite of loser-hood, the disease that all losers have, was my dentist. He had a photo of his whole family on his desk. They all wore matching clothes – in red and white, against a backdrop of snow-covered pine trees, in a Christmas pose. It was the first time I had seen a family all together for a thematic photograph. They were all blond, good-looking and smiling. Especially smiling, obviously.

That photo made me feel embarrassed: I had no family. I was American too, according to my papers, but in essence I was really a Latin product. It was on my face – and the rest of me – with all that insistent melanin in my skin. And I wore a jacket from an outlet to top it off. Almost all of my clothes were from outlets. The styles that would definitely be in the no-no columns of fashion magazines.

But there was hope. The photo seemed to suggest that if he was my dentist maybe one day I'd have teeth like his family's, and teeth like his family's could deliver me from all evil and make me of use to the world. Janis Joplin's good aspects plus my mother's good aspects, carefully selected. *Life is Good.*

Meanwhile, the molluscs in the sea at Copacabana drowned out the world in their crow-blue shells. And crows flew over the city of Lakewood, Colorado. Shell-blue crows.

Behind the headlands is a bay

FERNANDO WAS KNOWN as Horseshoe Chico when he arrived at the Peking Military Academy in the 1960s. In those days he had no way of imagining, not even in his wildest fits of creativity, Colorado, the red 1985 Saab, a girl called Vanja.

I never did find out where he got the codename from. How Fernando became Chico and got a Horseshoe to boot. It was one of the things he didn't tell me in the time we lived together, and wasn't among the papers that he let me examine, with a shrug – those insufficient letters and random notes that he kept in a wooden El Coto de Rioja wine crate in the back of his wardrobe, together with manuals for electrical appliances, old photos, an incomplete deck of cards and some expired coupons.

But he told me that shortly after disembarking in China and being greeted by an official retinue, in January 1966, he and the rest of the group of fifteen Brazilian Communist Party resistance fighters were invited to go to the opera.

The Peking Opera didn't seem like an opera. Not that Fernando knew anything about operas, but he imagined fat ladies singing in high voices, double-chins wobbling with the effort and fleshy white cleavages spilling over necklines (if someone were to prick the singer's breast with a pin there might be a magnificent operatic explosion, pieces of soprano falling onto the most expensive seats in the house). There in Peking, the spectacle was something else; a mixture of acrobatics, mime, dance, singing and theater. The actor-singers had painted masks over their faces and clothes covered in colors and sparkles and things dangling from their backs and hair and they sang in a completely different way to anything he had heard in his twenty-two years of life.

But Chico wasn't in Peking to watch performances, even though the opera, as long as it dealt with communist themes (anything else was subversive), was part of the revolutionary machine.

His journey to Mao Tse-Tung's China had begun ten months earlier, with a well-defined objective: to learn guerrilla warfare techniques together with fourteen other resistance fighters.

From Brasilia, where he lived, he had gone to São Paulo and then to Rio de Janeiro, where he spent some time trying to cover his own footsteps, and from there he had gone on to Paris, where he did the same, and then on to Peking.

Like others, he was convinced, as he would tell me later – me, who was so far removed from that whole story – that the military dictatorship in Brazil could be overthrown only if the people took up weapons. Elections? A possibility that didn't exist. The path of peaceful transition wasn't a path. The revisionists could say what they wanted: the fact was that parties would splinter and new parties, who believed in the people's armed struggle, would come into being and a long war to free the Brazilian people would ensue. It would take place above all in the countryside, its initial strategy being guerrilla warfare.

Hence the course in Peking: in the name of the people's war. In the name of the communist revolution in South America's largest country, following the Chinese example. And while Horseshoe Chico was learning guerrilla warfare techniques in China, the Brazilian Armed Forces were learning techniques for fighting the Domestic Enemy, including more and better torture methods, in the United States and Europe. And nowadays everyone knows about it all. But things have a distinctive face when you are living through the post-things years. When you were born so many years later. When you need people to enlighten you, to explain, to tell you that the things that seem so obvious in retrospect were obvious at the time too. The ugly truths went to the restroom and touched up their makeup. (At school, during Brazilian history lessons, everything was tedious, distant and slightly implausible. I watched the pigeons outside as the teacher was saying that during the 1960s. That during the 1970s. The 1970s for me were *That 70s Show* on the channel that showed foreign TV programs.)

Chico was good with weapons.

He was also good with women.

Both had appeared in his life very early. He had studied target-shooting in the interior of his home state of Goiás when he was still an adolescent. He was a natural. There was some kind of meta-physical union between him and the target. The bullet obeyed. The bullet knew resistance was futile.

Around the same time he fell in love with the first prostitute of his life, at the exact instant in which she took his hand and placed it on her cleavage. He asked her to marry him. She smiled at him in a half benevolent, half this-is-nothing-new-to-me way, and asked: how old are you? Seventeen. Liar, she said. I swear, he lied. And she didn't say anything else. That wasn't anything new to her either. In fact, most things were nothing new to her and everything was more of the same. Including kids who lied that they were seventeen when it was obvious that they were fifteen, if that.

He didn't actually say *prostitute*. He just described her one day, after a few beers, as a girl who worked in one of those places where there are girls, and my imagination filled in the rest, fishing meanings out of his silence, hanging in the air like those speech balloons in cartoons. He said he liked her, and I pictured her cleavage and thought it may really have been like that, just as I have pictured some other things over the years. After all, if people didn't provide me with details, I had the moral right to provide them myself.

At any rate, unfortunately, Horseshoe Chico's two talents didn't always agree to live in harmony in his future. Back then he was just Fernando, a kid who was full of energy and talked non-stop, useful qualities when he entered the University of Brasilia to study geography and got involved in the People's Action movement. He went to jail once or twice too. But he didn't learn to keep his mouth shut and watch the proud genesis of the Brazilian Economic Miracle (which was only miraculous for a while, and not for everyone, as he explained to me, but there was no question about it: everyone knew how painful, intensely painful, often mortally painful it was to challenge the military-uniformed status quo).

Almost four decades later, he still knew Chairman Mao's words off by heart: When the enemy advances, withdraw. When he stops, harass. When he tires, strike. When he retreats, pursue.

Not that things of this sort were still part of his life when I went to live with him almost four decades later.

Everything had a price. Doing something. Not doing something. Advance, withdraw, stop, harass, pursue.

Everything already had a price when he was commando-crawling through the frozen mud in Peking, during the training that was supposed to take six months and ended up taking over a year. It had a price when he attended night classes in political theory, interpreted by two Chinese comrades whom he secretly nicknamed Ping and Pong – a vice of the good humor that, back then, was almost an illness and wouldn't let go of him under any circumstances, not even on the coldest night of the Chinese winter and with serious subjects under discussion.

Everything already had a price when, on the journey back, the group of fifteen resistance fighters broke up in order to return to Brazil.

Saying that everything already had a price already had a price.

Chico entered Brazil across the Bolivian border, on foot, after passing through Europe. He stopped off in several Brazilian cities. He visited his mother in Goiânia, his widowed seamstress mother who was infinitely worried about the things her son was involved in and there was no point in him saying, in his best Maoist tone of voice, that he was doing it for her too. I'd rather you got a job, she would say, got married, gave me a couple of grandkids (not Maoists, she might have added), had barbeques (idem) on Sundays and didn't disappear without a word for so long.

She didn't know about the weapons, or Peking, and only suspected that her son's disappearances had something to do with politics. Worse than that, with communists, those bearded, inflamed men. She didn't know her son was one of them. Beard notwithstanding.

Chico met afterwards with the party leaders, worked in a country town in Bahia for a while and arrived in São João do Araguaia, in the state of Pará, on a summer's day, three years after boarding that plane to Peking.

Pará was a whole country. It was the size of a country. Pará was almost big enough for two Frances. Three Japans. Two Spains and a bit. More than one thousand, six hundred Singapores. In that vastness in Brazil's north, to which Brazil itself was oblivious, lived two million people when Chico set foot there for the first time.

It rained on the land, which was muddy and slippery, where shoes sank in and became stuck and came up sporting extra clods of mud on their soles when he lifted his feet.

It rained on the river, the Araguaia, the "River of the Macaws."

It rained on the forest: the wild, superhuman Amazon, which the communists believed would be a friend of the rebels, hell for the Armed Forces – an area fertile for planting subversion, as an army report would conclude.

The rain made Chico's clothes stick to his body, his hair to his forehead.

He glanced to one side and even though it wasn't one hundred percent appropriate at the time he decided to have a chuckle at the water dripping from the straight black hair of the young woman the guerrillas had come to collect in Xambioá, along with him, to take to that piece of nowhere where they were now arriving, strangers to one another, strangers to everyone else, strangers to the place, strangers, period.

He decided to laugh at the forest's thick rain drooping from her eyelashes, which made her blink a lot.

And she ended up laughing too, even if it wasn't one hundred percent appropriate at the time. She laughed at the dirty, worn t-shirt stuck to the thin kid's chest, and laughed because she didn't know anything: where she was, what exactly she was going to do there under the generic name of guerrilla training, where that thin kid was from. His hands were calloused. His arms were firm. Her hands were the elegant hands of a student from Rio, much more accustomed to books than to the jungle. She had smuggled some nail polish and nail polish remover with her in her bag. And a wad of cotton.

The young woman would discover that Chico knew how to use a hoe. That he was good with weapons.

And other things.

When the enemy advances, withdraw. When he stops, harass. When he tires, strike. When he retreats, pursue.

The young woman went by the codename Manuela. She had left Rio de Janeiro not knowing her final destination. When she arrived in the forest, she was given a large knife and a revolver. She would live in a crude shack together with a group that included the thin kid. It was the Faveira guerrilla base, Detachment A.

She would learn to sleep in a hammock, use a revolver and work the land. Her elegant hands would cease to be elegant. The nail polish and nail polish remover would never be used. She would help set up a small school in a nearby village and would start to teach there. She would grow fond and then very fond of the thin kid, who wasn't a kid, as he was twenty-five, two years older than her (fine, but he looked like a kid).

One day he told her about Peking, the frozen mud, the children playing in the snow, the opera, the farms and factories that he had visited (fine, but he still looked like a kid).

Deep in the forest, their neighbors were squatters: people who had fled the drought in Brazil's northeast, which lacked the wealth that fell here in abundance – the rainwater that muddied the ground, that stuck to the soles of Chico's worn shoes and that ran from Manuela's damaged, glamourless hair, falling as only Amazonian rain knows how to fall. Real *rain* rain, spilling all over the word, over every letter, over all of the preconceived ideas that you might have of rain, flooding them, warping them, drenching them and leaking through the cracks, showing you that if until that point you had referred to some other meteorological phenomenon as rain, you would have to rethink. Reconsider.

The squatters would arrive and occupy a piece of land in the middle of that no man's land. They would fell some trees, build a hut to live in and stay on.

The squatters thanked the rain for the rain; they thanked the rain gods, any thing or being, imaginary or not, physical or meta-physical in nature, that meant this: water in excess, the land on which to catch it.

★ ★ ★

A little over a year from then, General Médici affixed a bronze plaque to a tree trunk in the municipality of Altamira, inaugurating the great highway, which would go down in history as the most monumental public work conceivable by the military regime. The plaque said: *On these banks of the Xingu, deep in the Amazon jungle, the President of the Republic begins the construction of the Trans-Amazonian Highway, a historic start to the conquest of this gigantic green world.*

It was forty degrees that day. The general had hung the Brazilian flag from a tree (everything was improvised in those parts, it seemed) and listened to a military band play the national anthem, after being greeted by the three thousand inhabitants of Altamira. Later, the felling of a 160-foot tree marked the beginning of work on the future highway. The president was deeply moved.

His transport minister was also happy. He had an apple of his eye and the apple of his eye was a bridge: in addition to the highway slicing through Brazil from the Atlantic to the Peruvian border, in the southeast of the country Colonel Andreazza was building a structure, planned almost a century earlier, over Guanabara Bay to connect the cities of Rio de Janeiro and Niterói. The bridge had an enormous advantage over the highway: it would be finished. Better yet, the work wasn't inaugurated in the middle of the jungle, but amid civilization, and in the presence of two of the most civilized exponents of the civilized world possible: Queen Elizabeth II and Prince Philip.

A lot of people died during the construction of the Rio-Niterói Bridge. Legend has it that the dead stayed there, at the bottom of the bay, and the bridge was built over their bodies. If this is true, anyone driving over it is crossing a sad informal cemetery where cadavers rub shoulders with fish and concrete. The rumbling of the traffic overhead and the slight vibration of the heavy structure reaches their impotent, deafened ears. In their interrupted thoughts echo memories of the salty smell of the sea and the salty smell of the bay's humid air, crisscrossed by gulls and planes. With or without legends, the bridge was completed, with all the boring into the ocean floor and other monumentalities befitting the largest country in South America.

In Altamira, the tree trunk with the plaque commemorating the inauguration of the Trans-Amazonian Highway is known as the "President's Tree". There is some vegetation growing over it. Nearby is the municipality of Medicilância, but most of the population doesn't know who Médici was.

To me, he was (yet) another name in a history book, on a list of past presidents that we had to memorize. Someone who had called the shots in Brazil when my mother was still a child. When I wasn't even an idea, or a wish, or a danger, when I wasn't even holding a number waiting for someone to say off you go, it's your life now, it starts in five minutes.

It was as if Fernando and I were from different countries.

In forty years, an unimaginable number of things can happen. A fraction of them actually do. People are born, die, sing songs called "Me & Bobby McGee", don't sing them, more people are born, more people die, several disappear from the map without a trace. Trans-Amazonian highways inaugurated with great pomp are never finished, and the size of the wound can even be seen from outer space. Jeep drivers and motor cyclists often travel it in pursuit of mud and excitement. National football teams become three-time world champions, then four-time world champions, then five-time world champions, knowing that it still isn't everything and that history goes on. Eclipses take place. Tidal waves, earthquakes and hurricanes stir up many parts of the planet. Amazon forests start being cleared, non-governmental organizations emerge in their defense. Amazon forests continue being cleared to the order of one Belgium a year, basically for cattle farming. The miracle of the transubstantiation of forest into beef. (Soy? It too is transubstantiated. It is exported and becomes cattle fodder in rich countries.)

In forty years, girls called Evangelina appear in the world. They grow up in front of the sea in Copacabana. They suspect almost nothing. They have never seen eclipses. They have never witnessed tidal waves or earthquakes or hurricanes. Nor do they dream of moist Amazon forests where communist guerrillas once ventured, got wet, got dirty, fell in love, fired guns, got shot, were taken prisoner, hauled off to torture sessions and then buried here and there after they were dead.

And one fine day, deep in the innocence of youth, one of those blue Rio de Janeiro days, far from Altamira and São João do Araguaia, one of those days when the city wakes up and looks in the mirror and decides OK, today I'm going to be postcard perfect, on a day like this the mother of one such Evangelina goes to her daughter, calmly and seriously, and tells her something.

It starts like this:

Vanja, let's go out for an ice-cream.

Vanja leaps up from the front of the television. She pushes the button to turn off the set, which is already quite old and has a purplish smudge in the upper left-hand corner. It is as if it were growing ill, the poor TV. One day the purplish smudge is going to spread across the entire screen and the televised world will be uniformly purple.

Suzana, her mother, doesn't say much. They go out for an ice-cream. Vanja wants one of the new flavors, that caramelized milk one coated in chocolate and almonds. It is one of the most expensive, but Suzana says OK. (Strange. Vanja is suspicious.)

The two of them walk down to the beach promenade. They pass the beggar who lives on the corner of Rua Duvivier with his dog. The dog wags its tail. Vanja likes the dog. Suzana doesn't. Suzana belongs to that percentage of humankind that prefers cats to dogs and John Lennon to Paul McCartney.

There's something I need to tell you, says Suzana, when they sit on a bench facing the beach, the afternoon stretching their elastic shadows towards the sea. The sea has a magnet that attracts things, and people, and their shadows. Sometimes it regurgitates remains. Sometimes it doesn't.

Vanja is eleven. Suzana, thirty years older.

In a little paper bag is a jumble of names and words: *Albuquerque, Copacabana, London, Araguaia, LIFE. IS. GOOD. Amazon Colorado Guerrilla. Texas. American Boyfriend Nowhere.* Some of the words have to do with the present, others come from the past, others may belong to some future. They're there, tangled. It is a little paper bag that Vanja is going to take, unwittingly, in her suitcase of important things, when she travels back to the country where she was born and where the slogan is: life is good. The words and names in the

46

paper bag slowly detach from Suzana, belong to her less and less. So much so that she doesn't even mention them, although she knows they are there.

The important thing that she needs to tell her daughter is the only entirely predictable one, except that it is going to happen a little before its time. She explains. Talks. Then listens. She answers all questions. The questions are neverending, until they end. And with them the postcard-perfect afternoon and the need for answers.

Everything is going to be the same as before, Suzana says, after a time. Vanja wants to dive down to the ocean floor where strangely-colored molluscs live strange lives.

That night, Vanja and her mother don't say goodnight.

Can I sleep in your bed? asks Vanja.

Suzana says yes. At bedtime, she is wearing a white t-shirt without a bra and Vanja notices her nipples beneath the fabric. She raises her hands to her own chest. Almost nothing, yet, besides a slight swelling that she isn't sure if it really exists or if it is her imagination. She thinks her mother is beautiful, even if she has wrinkles around her eyes and the skin under her chin is beginning to get a little loose. She hugs her mother, with all those wrinkles, with folds of fat in undesirable places, when they lie down to sleep.

Everything is going to be the same as before.

Nothing is going to be the same as before and they know it.

My mother explained everything to me that day, with our shadows stretching out in front of us on the Copacabana beach promenade, towards the sea, at the entrance to the bay. Behind the headlands is a bay that appears to have been painted by the supreme painter-architect of the world, God, our Lord, (said Father Fernão Cardim, the Portuguese Jesuit priest, five centuries earlier).

My mother spoke calmly, carefully and seriously, and I put away the information like an item of clothing that you only use from time to time – a scarf, for example, in Rio de Janeiro – but which you know is there, at the back of the wardrobe, waiting for you.

She knew I needed that information. And she would never have forgiven herself if she hadn't told me first-hand what would soon be evident and self-explanatory. If I became aware of the facts not through her but through her disease, that inconvenient visitor sitting on the couch talking about unpleasant matters. That fountain of faux pas. It would be a kind of betrayal if the disease were to call me aside and say, with a glass of whisky in its hand: hey, you there, did you know . . . ?

My mother always answered all of my questions, so that any censorship was up to me: if I didn't want to know something, all I had to do was not ask. It wasn't always an easy decision. At times I would have preferred not to have all that autonomy regarding my own maturity. I would have preferred that certain choices had already been made at the factory and came with a sticker indicating the appropriate age group. Like at the movies. But my mother was my mother.

And that's the way it was, until the following year. I turned twelve. My breasts suddenly sprang out under my blouse, like employees late for work. My mother died as she had said she would, and it didn't take long as she had told me it wouldn't, and afterwards nothing was the same as before, as we both knew it wouldn't be.

★ ★ ★

It was in the month of July. And if the following year was displaced, there wasn't anything strange about that. There was a struggle going on, an internal battle: not to feel sorry for myself, in spite of all the sighs of "poor little thing" that I heard coming from heedless mouths.

I didn't feel poor or little. Something had happened, and the thing had two different appearances depending on which way you looked at it. My mother had also told me all of this.

It could be an antediluvian monster of sadness, something solid and unbearably heavy, with paws of lead, breath reeking of sulfur and beer, something that grabbed and silenced me, that reduced me to a heart that kept beating for lack of any other alternative. I could drag around a pair of bureaucratic feet and a pair of bureaucratic eyes, staring into space, my clothes hanging somewhat crooked on my body and greasy hair flopping across my forehead.

Or it could be something that happened among the myriad of things that happen all over the world in every instant, and at the same time there are traces of snow among the cactuses on a mountain in New Mexico, and a child in Jaipur drops a plate on the ground and the plate breaks, and a cat sneezes in Amsterdam and an ant loses its balance on a leaf in the Australian outback and kids graffiti a mural in Rio or in New York or in Bogotá. And my life would go on because I was the boss of it, not it of me.

Or maybe it was none of the above and I just needed a niche of quietness, of things not happening, a long, lasting moment, a moment that was the size of several moments, as many as necessary, that allowed me to be quiet, without having to name the things that I didn't want to name.

To stay there. Still. As if I had become a vase of plastic flowers on a shelf. The sort that requires no care at all. The sort that has no beauty, quality, singularity, scent, nothing. Something that can exist in the world with the courtesy of reciprocal indifference: I won't get in your hair if you don't get in mine.

And at school people were kind and helpful and looked at me with charity-tea eyes. And I'd walk past them and maybe they wondered what I was thinking, never imagining that I wasn't thinking anything. That I didn't want to think anything. That I didn't want their cards or flowers, or to be let off tests; that all I wanted was to pretend I was transparent, and if possible for them to pass right through me without even noticing.

I went to live with Elisa, my mother's foster sister, and she got it. She was the only one. Elisa let me lose as much weight as I wanted, sleep as much as I wanted and have as much insomnia as I wanted. Elisa let me not talk as much as I wanted. And she let me celebrate my thirteenth birthday with our octogenarian neighbors and then take a piece of cake to the beggar and his dog on the corner of Rua Duvivier. I squatted down next to the beggar and his dog and I noticed that the beggar had brown eyes and the dog had green eyes and in the eyes of both were things I had never read about in encyclopedias.

Elisa helped me when, at a given moment, I said, I want to call Fernando.

What Fernando, she asked, forgetting who he was and thus unaware of the importance that he had come to have in my life.

Fernando, my mother's ex-husband, I said.

★ ★ ★

No one knew Fernando's whereabouts. Someone thought he still lived in the United States, where he delivered pizzas or perhaps worked in a lunch bar selling Amazonian hamburgers. Or whatever it was that Brazilian immigrants did in the United States. Maybe he played golf or went skiing in his spare time. Maybe he wore a floral shirt in Miami or designer sunglasses in Los Angeles. Someone thought they had seen him just the other day on Leme Beach (looking older, pot-bellied).

A whole network of contacts, of Joe-Blow-who-knows-so-and-so's-brother-Joe-Schmoe-who-was-Fernando's-friend, was established. Half of Copacabana Beach was now mobilized in search of Fernando.

It couldn't be that hard to locate him, and he was the person – the only person – who could help me. Even almost two decades after he and my mother had broken up, and she had disappeared from his life, as she liked to do with all men.

It was a question of personal responsibility. My personal responsibility. And the inclusion of Fernando as a character in a story that at first had nothing, or almost nothing, to do with him. But which ended up being as much his as it was mine.

One fine day his name came up like that, an image gate-crashing a dream, and the memory that I didn't have came in its wake. Where might Fernando be, Fernando from the old days, whose face, to be honest, I couldn't remember (nor did I have any way to), who might he be today, how old might he be?

The network of informants closed in on him. Fernando was fifty-something and lived in Lakewood, a suburb of Denver, Colorado, far from the sea, from all beaches, in the west of the United States of America.

I looked it up on the map. I liked the name Colorado. It was a rectangular state flanked by other rectangular states. On the map, there were fungus-shaped mountains crossing Colorado from north to south. Green shadows indicating forests and a large brown smudge indicating the plains. To get to the ocean and its shells I could go to California or the Gulf of Mexico. It looked a little far.

Elisa argued with me, then she stopped arguing. We hadn't had any contact with Fernando for such a long time. Yes, my mother had been married to him, but she was ridiculously young when they tied the knot. And I needed to think, think hard. Whether or not my objective was reasonable, so to speak. But at one point she looked me straight on, in the eyes, and sighed.

My great-grandmother had her first baby at the age of thirteen, I told her.

I hope you don't intend to do the same.

At my age, my mother already knew how to drive, I said. She learned in her dad's pickup. I mean your dad's. Both of your dad's. I mean.

Someone got Fernando's address, but no one managed to get his phone number. From the look of things, he wasn't in the phone book. Maybe he didn't have a phone? So I wrote a letter, hoping he still lived at 94 Jay Street.

Before opening the envelope, Fernando had no idea of the identity of the person who owned the hand behind the round handwriting, with balls instead of dots over the i's. And the surname was too common to immediately set in motion the cogs of the past and the gears of recognition in his memory and produce an experimental fruit.

Or maybe he was bowled down by instant recall, that leaped up in his chest and caused him to raise his hand and lift his Colorado Rockies cap in a gesture of reverence, revealing a perfectly circular bald patch. I never found out. He never told me.

On the envelope with green and yellow trim around the edges I wrote our names and addresses – his, Fernando's, the addressee, in his house in Lakewood, Colorado, and mine, Evangelina, the sender's. The letter would be posted in Brazil, the distant South American cousin that had so little in common with its North American cousin, except for the quirks of their continental dimensions.

I took the green and yellow trim of the Brazilian envelope to the post office on Rua Ronald de Carvalho, watched to make sure it was stamped properly, paid and started waiting right then and there, resting my chin on my interlaced fingers, my nose almost touching the greasy glass partition.

Next, said the post office employee in a slack voice, stretching the "e" over my head, beyond my anxiousness, and directing a pair of dead-fish eyes at the man behind me in the queue.

Among the echoes of her lazy vowel one could hear: go home, silly girl, your letter's been posted.

Ursus arctos horribilis

IN AUGUST, I started going with Fernando every now and then to the Denver Public Library, where he worked as a security guard. We would walk a little way, catch the bus, then walk some more to the block delimited by Broadway, Bannock Street and 13th and 14th avenues. The red 1985 Saab stayed in the garage. Parking was expensive near the library.

I quickly discovered that I hated reading books in English (my mother's lessons hadn't included books), that it was really quite difficult, that speaking and understanding a language reasonably well are no guarantee of instant fluency or pleasure in reading, and that I would have to do it.

I'd have to do it anyway, at school, so I might as well try to arrive there a little less green. I spoke English. I understood English. And people would have to take their hats off to me.

I chose books I didn't know by their titles. I set several aside before the end of the first chapter. Those that interested me I took home and continued reading when I wasn't helping with the cleaning or in the kitchen (where little help was required because almost everything that Fernando bought was half-ready or frozen), or skating around the neighborhood or just watching TV – my favorite activity.

Watch TV, said Fernando. It's good for picking up English.

His TV set didn't have purple smudges. I watched TV feverishly, trying to catch every bit of slang. After an hour I'd have a headache. Reading wasn't a good pain killer. Sometimes washing pots and vacuuming the living room was. Cleaning the windows.

I liked cleaning the windows of Fernando's house and was sorry there weren't more of them; it would have been great if the house were floor-to-ceiling glass. The noise of the moist paper on the glass was comforting. It was of the order of practical things, of useful, honest things without anything grandiose about them. It was a good, simple activity. My mother would have approved. She would have cleaned the windows too, if she had been there.

I imagined her married to Fernando – it was a little difficult, the image, but I tried hard and something came of it. Thinking about my mother and Fernando married was almost like watching a film: two entirely strange people acting out a scene in a time when I didn't even exist, with strange gestures and wearing clothes that were already out of fashion, until a director said cut. Two people who lived together for the duration of a film screening.

A few times a week Fernando would go out, when he wasn't working at the library, to clean people's houses. A good way to make some extra money, he explained. I spend three hours cleaning someone's house and I take home seventy dollars. Tax-free.

And no one bothers me. I'm my own boss and the whole thing is between me and the carpet, me and the windows, me and the bathroom sinks and toilets and tiles. Not bad.

I thought Fernando didn't like people. As a security guard, at the library, he always maintained a professional, distant air – which mustn't be too hard, I guess, when you are a security guard. People don't tend to come up to you to chat. His uniform commanded respect, official-looking and imbued with power, and his strong arms and surly face completed the picture.

I wondered what Fernando thought about for hours and hours on end, just standing there, not talking to anyone. At other times, he had carpets, windows and toilets for company. He had his own equipment: a vacuum cleaner, the most efficient products, a kit developed through years of experience. He would put everything in the back of the red Saab and drive off for another few hours of not interacting with humanity.

For me, considering all this, his relationship with my mother left the realm of films and became a cloud of ectoplasm exhaled from a medium's nostrils. That is, a phenomenon I had heard of but couldn't really believe in. My mother liked parties and people; she liked cooking for lots of friends and having house guests; she liked dancing. She liked sticking her head out the window of her Fiat 147 and singing "Me & Bobby McGee" at the top of her lungs. How could she ever have taken an interest in this guy?

I asked the question in a bold gesture at dinner (it was that New Orleans-style food, which came pre-mixed and seasoned in a little box and all you had to do was add water and boil it for twenty-five minutes and I was already an expert at it): Have you changed a lot since you were married to my mother?

He shrugged.

No one changes. You just get used to things. You adapt.

He said it without bitterness. Fernando came across as being exactly what he appeared to be. Which could mean two things: that he was exactly what he appeared to be. Or that he was a talented liar, the worst kind – the sort that lie to themselves, with so much conviction and effort that they end up believing it, and then when they tell other people their lies they think they are actually telling the truth.

But this was a supposition made months later. I still didn't know Fernando well enough to think anything except that what he had said at dinner was hogwash. That my mother would never have taken an interest in him if he had been, at thirty-six, the same man that he appeared to be at fifty-something. That the whole story that no one changes, etc., was just something you trotted out in conversation. That one of them had certainly changed, and a lot, and I suspected it hadn't been my mother.

But she wasn't there to confirm it, so I stayed quiet. Another thing she had taught me was to mind my own business.

Which I followed to the letter with Fernando.

In the beginning, at least.

When Fernando called Elisa's house and asked to speak to me, he had probably had time to rehearse his words. He had had time to chew over, swallow and digest the information in my letter, which was a lot, and serious.

I imagined him arriving home at the end of a normal afternoon and getting his correspondence from the letterbox in his little garden – one of those square letterboxes that I had only seen in cartoons.

An envelope with dangerously Brazilian green and yellow trim. Inside it, news about the woman he had been married to for six years and whom he hadn't seen or spoken to or heard of for so long that maybe he wondered if she had really existed.

She had really existed, said my letter, but didn't anymore, at least not in the way we tend to understand existence in terms of the spongy substance that we carry around on the ends of our necks. I could think of at least one way in which my mother continued to exist a little, and to certify it all I had to do was touch my own skin. Nothing particularly transcendental or esoteric or mystical, no ectoplasm-sneezing mediums: my own skin. Me. I was her, a little, wasn't I?

Maybe Fernando thought similarly. He called me and said he was very sorry to hear the news and asked how I was with a forwardness that was somewhat excessive, perhaps rehearsed. Then he told me the barest essentials about his life, where he worked (as a security guard at the Denver Public Library), that he lived alone and that yes, I could stay with him for a while until – until things were resolved, or moving along.

Neither of us knew how things were going to be resolved, or even how they were going to move along, or how we were going to move them along, because without a gesture they would most certainly stay the way they were. But I would attend the public school in Lakewood for a while and he would help me as much as he could.

Depending on what happened, well, depending on what happened I would return to Brazil later. To Elisa's place in Copacabana. It was curious how the central people in my life were now all peripheral. My mother's foster sister. My mother's ex-husband.

I don't know if Fernando could have guessed, at that moment, during that trans-hemispheric phone call, how much he was capable of. He would be surprised. But the future was (and is, and always will be) a mutating thing, the fruit of successive forks in the road, and I was already beginning to suspect that making plans was an embarrassingly useless habit.

I have a little money, I said. My mother left it. It isn't a lot, but I'll be able to help out.

Where one eats, there's always room for one more, he said. The school is public. We'll get by.

You're brave, Elisa told me, when I hung up. And I must be crazy.

I looked at her and didn't say anything but I thought lots of things. You didn't have to be brave to do what I was doing. In fact, you'd have to be brave to stay where I was, a fixed point in space, nurturing like a sick little animal the idea that nothing had changed, that nothing was different, walking along the same streets, keeping up the same habits, faking myself.

What if I went with you. I'll go with you, she said.

She glanced sideways, clasped her hands together.

It isn't possible, I can't go with you. What about my work? I think it'd be better if you waited a while longer. A year or two.

I didn't say anything.

I now know that if I hadn't done what I did I would have turned to stone in that life, a bone that heals crooked. That was the window that pre-empted the impulse, the right moment to jump unseen into the cargo train as it passed, if that were the only way to take off into the world, and if I had to take off into the world. Nothing about it even remotely resembled irresponsibility or courage or spirit of adventure.

It wasn't an adventure. It wasn't a holiday or fun or a pastime or a change of scenery; I was going to the United States to stay with Fernando with a very specific objective in mind: to look for my father.

A person looking for something or someone basically has two possible outcomes on the horizon: they can find what they are looking for or not find what they are looking for.

I knew this. But when I made my decision and wrote the letter to Fernando and waited for his phone call with my only suitcase ready and then got on the plane that would fly in a north-westerly direction, at that moment finding or not finding my father was still just that, two possibilities of the same size, and I would deal with whatever I had to deal with when the time came.

Elisa sighed.

I can't go with you.

Then she cried a little.

Your mother should have got back together with Fernando when you were born. Fine, she didn't want to be with your father, she didn't have to stay with him, it was just a fling, you know? But Fernando was a nice guy. I'm sure she liked him.

She cried a little more.

Your mother was silly. She always found fault with everyone. No one was good enough, no one was right. That's why she ended up alone.

And she hugged me, and her smell had Vibrant Notes of Peach, Gold Raspberry and Patchouli, as explained in the commercial for the perfume she was wearing. I saw it all the time on the purple TV.

Then she took my head in her hands and brushed the hair off my forehead.

Fernando will take good care of you. He's a nice guy. He always was a nice guy. Your mother should have got back together with him. I'm going to save up to come visit you at Christmas.

In the years following that summer, I met entire families of Latin immigrants, legal and illegal, who made their living as cleaners.

I never met Maria Isabel Vasquez Jimenez, but I heard about her, the seventeen-year-old Mexican girl who died of heat stroke while picking grapes in the fields of California, without anyone offering her water or shade. It was in the month of May. The year, 2008. Maria Isabel's core body temperature reached 108 degrees.

Fernando had been a legal resident of the United States for almost thirty years, but he had never applied for citizenship, unlike my mother. I asked why and he told me that it was because it was a laborsome process. He made some extra money cleaning for seventy dollars. Each cleaning job took two to three hours.

In Rio de Janeiro, the cleaning lady who came to clean our apartment in Copacabana once a week earned half that and was there from eight in the morning until four in the afternoon. She would arrive with fresh bread from the bakery, for which my mother would reimburse her. She would stop cleaning to have lunch in the kitchen listening to the radio and then she'd wash the dishes and make a cup of coffee and smoke a cigarette and gossip and take a quick nap. Every now and then she'd sew a button back onto my clothes or let down a hem (my mother was a disaster with a needle and thread). She'd come by bus from São Gonçalo and the trip took about an hour. Before starting to work for private clients like us, she used to clean the parking lot of a shopping center in Barra da Tijuca, where her monthly wages couldn't even buy her a dress. The sun was hot. I don't know what her core body temperature was, but she ended up having to quit. She was sixty years old.

After examining Maria Isabel Vasquez Jimenez's body, the doctors discovered that she was two months pregnant. She was picking grapes for wine.

At the airport in Rio, Elisa and I ate *pães de queijo*, the mini cheese buns, and drank *guaraná*. She was admirably strong until twelve seconds before we had to say goodbye.

The Federal Police officer asked for my authorization to travel and my birth certificate.

Your father lives in the United States, he confirmed.

Yes, I said, and in principle I wasn't lying.

He's Brazilian, the officer confirmed once again. I don't know why he kept repeating things that were in the documents: I was the daughter of Suzana and Fernando, both Brazilians, she an American citizen too, dead a year earlier, hence my trip to the United States. It was all in the documents and he asked me to confirm it all before wishing me a good trip.

Officially, Fernando was my father and legal guardian. When my mother fell pregnant to my real father, an American, she disappeared from his life, and when I was born in New Mexico she phoned her ex-husband Fernando, who lived to the north in the state of Colorado, six hours away by car.

In those days he didn't live in Lakewood, but in Aurora, another Denver suburb. He drove down and registered me the next day as his daughter, in Albuquerque. He told my mother to take care of herself. Then he drove back. They had been divorced for four years and he possibly knew her well enough that she didn't have to explain anything:

That she didn't want any ties to her daughter's real father.

That she didn't want her daughter to grow up without a father's name on her birth certificate.

That she didn't dare ask anyone else.

That sometimes life was a bit complicated.

I have no idea what happened between the two of them after that. All the information I have is that later that same year, 1988, Fernando went to Albuquerque to spend Christmas with me and my mother. He stayed in the adobe house, which only had two rooms – mine and my mother's.

Maybe he slept on the living room couch.

The highways are an adventure in December in this part of the world. Fernando was on the road for much more than the usual six hours between cities on Interstate 25. There was snow and ice on the road.

He left behind Trinidad, former residence of Bat Masterson and, in those days, the world sex change capital thanks to the operations conducted by the famous Dr. Stanley Biber. He passed a sign saying WELCOME TO NEW MEXICO LAND OF ENCHANTMENT and in his rear-view mirror saw a sign saying WELCOME TO COLORFUL COLORADO, with the Sangre de Cristo Mountains to the west.

I don't know if, when he arrived in Albuquerque, I was in my room dreaming pint-sized dreams, dreams that were the size of my life, that fit easily through the bars of the crib. I don't know if he and my mother embraced with the force of how deeply they missed one another, or thought they missed one another, or needed to miss one another because missing often keeps you company. I don't know if he went to bed with her, or if she just made some soup or tea and they sat in front of the Christmas tree to sip the soup or tea and then she helped him spread some sheets and a blanket over the living room couch.

The following year he didn't go to Albuquerque at Christmas. And two years later my mother and I returned to Brazil. It was supposed to be for good.

In her case, it was.

A curious phenomenon happens when you have been away from home for too long. Your idea of what home is – a city, a country – slowly fades like a colorful image exposed to the sun on a daily basis. But you don't quickly acquire another image to put in its place. Try: act like, dress like, speak like the people around you. Use the slang, go to the "in" places, make an effort to understand the political spaces. Try not to be surprised every time you see people selling second-hand furniture and clothes and books from their garages (the sign on the street corner announces: garage sale), or the supermarkets offering tons of pumpkins in October and tolls for sculpting them, or corn mazes. Pretend that none of it is new to you.

Do it all, act like.

I met Brazilian immigrants who tried to forget they were Brazilian. They got themselves American partners, American children, American jobs, and stored the Portuguese language in some hard-to-access place in their throats and only took pride in their origins when someone spoke praisingly of samba or capoeira (the latter too, in its origin, the martial art of the displaced, of the expatriated, of those torn from their homes). Or the Gracie brothers' Brazilian jujitsu. Apart from these things, Brazil was crap. And getting worse and worse. Worse and worse. (Don't you read the news? Did you see what the drug lords did in São Paulo?)

In the beginning, I thought it was a survival strategy. Maybe it was. Or maybe it was just permeability. After a while, it is hard to remain unaffected. To keep dreaming in Portuguese when the other sixteen hours of the day you are surrounded by American co-workers, American sales assistants, the Mexican postman who talks to you in English, American radio stations, American TV.

Perhaps (another hypothesis) it was the disease of Latin American immigrants in the first world: the desperate need to embrace the rich country with all their might and say I want a piece. My story isn't just mine. It's yours too. For example: where does your cocaine come from? The meat on your barbecue? The illegal wood in your shelves? Your story isn't just yours. It's mine too. Our American dream. After all, America is a chunk of land that stretches from the Arctic Ocean down to Cape Horn, isn't it?

Although Brazilians have always positioned themselves very clearly in this story: hold on, we are not Hispanic immigrants. Take a look at our faces. We're actually quite different in terms of biotype and we don't speak Spanish. We speak Portuguese. POR. TU. GUESE. (At school, I had to put my ethnic group on a form. The options were: CAUCASIAN. HISPANIC. NATIVE AMERICAN. ASIAN. AFRICAN-AMERICAN. Where was I in all that?)

Perhaps (last hypothesis) it was all just cordiality. It isn't polite to speak in front of other people in a language they don't understand and to be a person they don't understand. One of the biggest complaints of American citizens who are opposed to immigration is that the immigrants don't learn English. But studies show, as Mr. Atkins taught us at school, that it is the opposite: English is assimilated very quickly, and the immigrants' mother tongues are slowly forgotten. It is a fact and Mr. Atkins left no room for doubt, as he hammered the table with his index finger. Mr. Atkins liked to hammer the table with his index finger, driving his statements into the world emphatically and forever.

Cordiality. Necessity. Shame. Curiosity. Ambition. Admiration. The desire to be equal. To belong. Whatever.

After you have been away from home for too long, you become an intersection between two groups, like in those drawings we do at school. You belong to both, but you don't exactly belong to either. Your memory of home is always old, always out of date. People are listening to such-and-such a song all the time in Brazil: it plays on the nightly soap, it plays on the radio. Six months later you accidentally stumble across the song, like it, and its huge prior popularity feels like a kind of betrayal. It is as if people were telling each other secrets and you were always being surprised by old news. The people from group A consider you somewhat different because you also belong to group B. The people in group B eye you a little suspiciously because you also belong to group A. You are something hybrid and impure. And the intersection of the groups isn't a place, it is just an intersection, where two entirely different things give people the impression that they converge.

For example, I'd go buy a sandwich and would place my order as carefully as possible, remembering my mother's perfect English, arranging each vowel and consonant in my mouth with feng shui attention to detail. A few instants later the girl at the cash register would ask me where I was from. Damn: how is it that other people can hear your accent if you can't? My tongue was perfectly retro-flexed for my r's and touched the inside of my top front teeth ever so softly for my th's. What was missing?

Later I realized that life away from home is a possible life. One of many possible lives.

Timothy Treadwell decided to be a grizzly man and went to live in Katmai National Park, in Alaska. It lasted thirteen summers. In the end, he was killed and eaten by a bear. Tim's disfigured head was found at the camp site. His arm with the still-ticking watch. A piece of his spine. The remains of his girlfriend, Amie Huguenard, too. This happened a year after I arrived in the United States. I was a fourteen-year-old girl and he was a forty-six-year-old guy. A possible life and a possible death.

Fernando left home and went to study guerrilla warfare techniques in Peking, then he moved to the Faveira guerrilla base on the Araguaia River. This happened two decades before I was born. It was a possible life and a possible death, both deeply interconnected, like during Tim Treadwell's summers. Like during the last summer of Amie Huguenard, who was possibly thinking of leaving Tim and his black clothes and his Prince Valiant hair and his obsession with bears. Grizzlies. *Ursus arctos horribilis.*

Fernando had been so many places after leaving home that he could no longer remember the way back. Of course: home wasn't there anymore, therefore the way back couldn't be either. And it wasn't that home was everywhere now – no, that's for citizens of the world, those who travel for sport. For those who have never commando-crawled through the frozen mud in China and never run the risk of being devoured by bears in Alaska. It wasn't that home was everywhere: home wasn't anywhere.

We'll get by, Fernando told me over the phone.

My former classmates sent me emails from Rio de Janeiro, having forgotten the mourning period they had imposed on me when I was still among them. How are things in the United States? Are the guys really good-looking, with blond hair and blue eyes? Are you going to go to Disneyland? Are you going to go to Hollywood? Is it true that the kids take guns to school and every now and then go around shooting everyone? Is it true that people only eat hamburgers and pizza and only drink Coca-Cola? Is it true that American girls have really big boobs?

Aditi Ramagiri would ask me: What's it like in Brazil? Is it true that you live in the middle of the jungle? Is it true that it's really violent and dangerous, a nation of corrupt politicians and drug dealers? What language do you speak – Brazilian?

I'd ask Aditi Ramagiri: What's life like in India? Is it true that there's a river there where people throw their dead and bathe and wash their clothes, all at the same time? Is it true that your family decides who you're going to marry? What language do you speak – Indian?

We got by. I got by at school, in the first week, trying to act cool. And for some reason the other kids decided to think I was cool.

Rio de Janeiro? Cool! What the heck are you doing here, dude?

I couldn't say, well, dude, what I'm doing here, what the heck I'm doing here is trying to see if I can find my dad, he's got to be somewhere, my mom died a year ago and I'm living with her ex-husband who's my dad on my birth certificate but he isn't my real dad.

So I'd shrug and keep to myself but the other kids thought I was cool and Aditi Ramagiri, who was popular, thought I was cool and we became friends and she made me see how Jake Moore was a loser.

When I told her just half of my story (the maternal half) her eyes grew genuinely misty and she hugged me and thought I was even cooler. After all, it wasn't everyone whose life had the dramatic ingredient of having lost their mother at the age of twelve, and it wasn't every day that you had the opportunity to bring this dramatic ingredient into your life via a friend, without having to experience it first-hand.

Once I went to a debating championship with Aditi. She was on the school debate team and almost every weekend had to participate in these events, in which people had to argue consistently and coherently in favor of something even when they were really against it.

This time it was a private Catholic school in Littleton. I was outside the classroom with Aditi, waiting for her turn. Five kids arrived. An Asian boy and his friend, who wasn't Asian, sat next to me. In front of me sat an Asian girl with the strangest body shape I had ever seen. She was wide. Not fat, but wide. With a wide face. She was wearing a dress. Next to her was a black girl wearing a metal necklace with a crucifix hanging from it. On the other side was a white girl wearing a metal necklace with a pendant that I couldn't tell what it was.

Suddenly the Asian girl said OK, I was late to the last round of the debate because I had to use the bathroom! and someone told me there was a bathroom over by the lockers.

And the girl with the crucifix necklace said, there's a closer one.

And the Asian girl, shouting, said, I know! but they told me to go to the other one! so I went over to the lockers and it was a maze, and finally I found the bathroom! then, after I'd peed, I came out and saw two doors! there were two doors! the door I had come through and another one next to it! and the door I had come through didn't have a door handle on the inside and the other one was locked! I couldn't get out!

I wanted to say something. I looked around. But the one who spoke was Aditi.

I hate this school. It's scary.

Really? Why? We love it! Because we see Jesus everywhere and we're Catholic.

Well, to begin with, it looks like a kindergarten, and secondly, I keep thinking I'm going to hell, said Aditi.

We don't necessarily believe in hell.

Look at our necklaces! I've got a cross.

I've got the Holy Ghost.

I never did get what the Holy Ghost is, said Aditi.

Well, said the white girl. It's pretty complicated. It's like this: Jesus, God and the Holy Ghost are the same thing. That is, not even our most knowledgeable thinkers and philosophers can understand it properly.

For example, said her friend. Imagine an elephant with green spots. The elephant is Jesus, the elephant's soul is God, and the elephant's spots are the Holy Ghost.

The others laughed. That's not exactly what we believe in.

A week later I joined the ultimate frisbee team. I had never imagined such a sport even existed, but I discovered I had a surprising talent for it. It was played with one of those discs they used to call frisbees that we can't call frisbees anymore because some manufacturer registered the name.

How did you end up here, I heard myself asking as Fernando was fixing the toilet.

I had been putting off the question for a month. Four weeks, during which he made phone calls when he got back from work, looked up people he used to know whom he didn't know anymore, asked questions, moonlighted as a detective. He had hunches, suspected, supposed. And he didn't uncover anything worthy of note, not a smidgeon of a clue, no bread trail in the forest. Why do people have to cover up their former lives so well?

During those weeks we didn't speak much: about the past, about the present, about the future. When school started, in mid-August, I began to ask him for help with my homework. He was the available adult.

He would look at the math problems and scratch his head and sigh, and he'd say, I studied math in Portuguese, Vanja.

And I had to translate the problem; I had to help him first so that he could then help me.

The bulky finger of his bulky hand would underline the numbers, and in that domestic setting, sitting next to me at the table with the dirty dishes still in the sink, wearing reading glasses, Fernando seemed like an insect shedding its exoskeleton and revealing a soft, almost fragile interior.

I still didn't know what subjects I could broach with him. Maybe all subjects. I had twelve hundred pages of questions about my mother, about him and my mother, about my father and my mother, about New Mexico, about the scenes acted out before I was born. I wanted to know why people chopped and changed between lives like that, and changed cities, and changed countries, and took out new citizenships or didn't take out new citizenships. Why, in this chopping and changing, old loves dropped off the face of the earth, and old loves transubstantiated into friendships

73

dropped off the face of the earth. And why fathers dropped off the face of the earth.

Perhaps there was a tacit agreement between Fernando and me that a little silence was necessary for a while; that we had to be somewhat monastic and observe a kind of non-action. Maybe it was time for me to remodel myself; maybe I too had (must have had) that soft, albino interior that insects have under their exoskeletons. Maybe I needed to take that slimy interior and, after having managed to protect it from other people's fulminating pity, mould it now into some shape with which I could re-identify.

There were practical strategies for doing this. I had a pile of books in English on my bedside table, authors whose given names were always abbreviated to two (sometimes three) letters before the surname. And they weren't just JK or JRR or CS. The librarian suggested other initials. Big people's books, she said. As a result I also started reading poems, which were even more difficult, by the likes of WH, TS and WB, which at first seemed like a separate language within the English language – something ciphered, in code.

One day I came across a line at the end of a poem that said thousands have lived without love, not one without water. And I thought it made sense. I thought the poem made sense, even when it didn't, even when it was a tangle of words.

I read ferociously, like a trained athlete during the Olympics, and from these experiences extracted the mortar for that new exoskeleton. I also watched TV ferociously.

But the question popped out as Fernando was fixing the toilet and I was looking on, sitting on the edge of the bathtub.

I was there to offer help, as a scrub tech perhaps, but he didn't seem to need my help, so instead I offered him a question.

That question. How did you end up here?

I thought maybe he didn't want to talk about it. Fernando didn't seem like the kind of person who kept the past in colorful photo albums to show visitors. He didn't look at me.

Your mother didn't tell you.

My mother didn't tell me much about you. She didn't talk much about the things that had happened in her life before. Before me.

A few moments of silence.

I met your mother in London. I was working in a bar and one day she came in with her American boyfriend. They were on vacation. At some point she came up to the bar to get two more beers and she said you're not from here, your accent is different, and I decided I was going to steal her from her American boyfriend before I even knew that besides being American like him she was also Brazilian like me.

And did you steal her?

He looked at me. Don't flush it for an hour until it's dry.

OK.

Fernando left the bathroom and I followed him. He opened the fridge and took out a beer.

Those were hard times in London, he said. I wasn't there sightseeing. I was there because I couldn't stay in Brazil. That was way before you were born. You're lucky. Those were hard times.

He took a swig of beer. I opened the cupboard and got out the packet of extra-cheesy cheese crackers that were covered in a kind of dust that left my fingers dirty.

Want some?

He took a handful and dirtied his fingers with the extra-cheesy cheese cracker dust.

Of course I stole your mother from her American boyfriend. I went to great lengths. For him, things were guaranteed. She was his girlfriend, not mine. So I had to fight for her. And that's why I followed Suzana here to the United States.

It was the first time in a month that he had said my mother's name.

Later, you know how life is (no, I didn't know), you wake up one day and you're fifty years old and you've lost that urge to do things, to wander around, to look for a place in the world because the truth is that the world is a pretty fucking wild place. It's not worth it. It doesn't make any difference.

He took another swig of beer.

The doorbell rang. Fernando went to open it, responded in monosyllables for two minutes to something a woman was telling him. He came back with a pamphlet, which he tossed on the table and I read out of the corner of my eye, in simultaneous translation. *Does God really care about us? Will there ever be an end to war and suffering? What happens to us when we die? Is there any hope for the dead? How can I pray and be heard by God? How can I find happiness in this life?* There was a photo of an Arab with a moustache and a plump white man wearing glasses and a tie, both sitting with their legs crossed on an oriental rug, both smiling, nattering over an open Bible.

Fernando cleared his throat.

Sorry I said fucking. I've been meaning to tell you, I've been making some phone calls and I've managed to find an old friend of your mother's who lives in Santa Fé. She might be able to help us track down Daniel.

It was the first time in a month that he had said my father's name. Through the open window, I heard the woman with the God pamphlets talking to our neighbor, who had hair the color of fire and who was answering very loudly in her Hispanic English.

Fish

FERNANDO HAD A letter, just one, from Manuela, the young woman he had met on the Araguaia River. And whose name wasn't really Manuela, of course, just as his name wasn't really Chico. Her name was Joana. The letter was signed with an M.

It was from late 1971. Neither Chico or Manuela knew it, but a few months from then a guerrilla by the name of Pedro, who had left the Araguaia with his pregnant wife, would be arrested in Fortaleza trying to obtain a new copy of his ID.

Pedro was thinking about resuming his law degree. While being tortured by the Federal Police, he would invent things and switch names (the town of Xambioá, where the guerrillas also circulated, would become Shangri-La), but would end up dropping clues about the guerrillas' training centers. His torturers already knew, as he would say later, that the Brazilian Communist Party was present in the region.

He was to be the first casualty in the story of the repression of the guerrilla movement. He would attempt suicide in his cell, cutting the veins in his arms. But they wouldn't authorize him to die.

Pedro and his wife, known by the codename Ana, left the Araguaia because she had fallen pregnant. The Party's orientation was to get an abortion. She didn't accept it, and he decided to go with her. They left as fugitives, took a bus, got help from friends. After going underground in Fortaleza, it occurred to him to go down to the Department of Political and Social Order and apply for a new copy of his ID card.

The information they got from Pedro would circulate through the agencies of repression, until a dragnet of army, navy and air force agents was set up. Later versions, from the communists themselves, blamed Regina, another fighter who left the Bico do Papagaio region that same year and never returned, for having led the military to the guerrillas. She had supposedly told her family in São Paulo everything, and they had blown the whistle.

At any rate, with information from one or the other or both, Operation Fish I was born.

I read up on fish and found out that they don't sleep. I had never thought about it before, about how fish sleep. They don't. *They merely alternate between states of wakefulness and rest. The rest period consists of an apparent state of immobility, in which the fish maintain their balance with very slow movements. Because they don't have eyelids, their eyes are always open. Some species lie on the ocean floor or riverbeds, while smaller ones hide in holes so they won't be eaten as they are resting.*

And: *In 2003, Scottish scientists from the University of Edinburgh discovered that fish can feel pain* [citation needed]. Wikipedia.

In the case of the Brazilian Armed Forces, however, the fish that lent its name to the operation was merely to evoke the image of the dragnet. To bring in subversive fish. Red fish who wanted – what? To make Brazil into Cuba? (No, the Cuban Revolution had been based on the *foco* theory of guerrilla warfare, which had failed in Bolivia, Argentina and Peru. According to the Brazilian Communist Party, focalism underrated the importance of the Party, was based on individual acts of heroism and was thus idealistic and petty-bourgeois.)

The region is still known as Bico do Papagaio, even though other things have changed since then on the map of Brazil.

The name ("Parrot's Beak") comes from the shape of the Araguaia River as it flows into the Tocantins, where three Brazilian states meet. In the years that Chico and Manuela spent there, they were Pará, Maranhão and Goiás. They are now Pará, Maranhão and Tocantins, because of the reformulation of the states. But Bico do Papagaio is still there. The land has been flayed and the borders altered, but the rivers haven't changed course or dried up. The mountains are in the same place.

You go chop firewood in the forest, then bring it to the base, Comrade César told Manuela, a few days after they had arrived. It's physical training. You stay in shape and carrying firewood is like carrying weapons or the body of a wounded companion. And nobody'll think anything of it; we're just chopping firewood.

(What on earth were women doing getting caught up in politics, and becoming *guerrillas* to boot, in an era in which they were still expected to stay confined to the home and domestic life?

Communist whores. That was the nickname they heard in the torture sessions. Against the homeland there are no rights.)

At night, César would sometimes pick up a guitar and sing something by Noel Rosa. Chico didn't sing, as he was chronically tone-deaf, but he watched Manuela from afar. Manuela felt his moist stare within the walls of the hut, and it felt nice, magnetized, pointed – just as he pointed his guns at a target and never erred. Chico never erred, ever.

What are you doing here, girl? He went and sat by her in the clearing, where a camp fire was lit to keep the mosquitoes at bay.

The same as you.

You're so young.

And you're not?

Their hands were cracked and blistered. Their clothes were dirty and their skin covered in insect bites. The forest animals were making noise. The firewood that Manuela had chopped that morning crackled on the camp fire. The crackling was almost hypnotic. But Chico and Manuela wouldn't be hypnotized by the fire and its crackling, because their attention wasn't on the camp fire.

You're pretty, said Chico.

She laughed.

Stop kidding around.

I'm serious.

She looked at Chico, who had studied at the Peking Military Academy, who knew how to use (and make) weapons and would come to be one of the most skillful woodsmen in the detachment.

She said: You know what they say about Osvaldão, that he's immune to danger?

Yeah.

I think you must be too. I think it's thanks to people like him and you that this is all going to work out.

Osvaldão, the commander of Detachment B, the most popular leader among the guerrillas and adored by the locals too, wasn't immune to danger. When the military finished him off years later they hung his body from a helicopter so there would be no doubts. But who could have predicted this, at that point in time? Osvaldão seemed indestructible. He was a six-foot-tall black man and former boxing champion. He liked to help. He made friends.

At that point in time, before Pedro was captured and before the first military campaign on the Araguaia, everything was going to work out.

At that point in time, the Party believed the population was going to get involved. The 1969 resolution said: *There is no other alternative for Brazilians: to rise up in arms against the backward army and the imperialist Yankees or forever have to endure the country's reactionaries and foreign looters.*

But why that, Fernando? Why go into the middle of the forest, far from everything, without contact with anyone, I asked one day. Weren't you studying to be a geographer? Why didn't you stay there, studying to be a geographer in Brasilia, it was in Brasilia, wasn't it? You could have gotten involved in politics there in Brasilia, couldn't you?

Fernando looked at me. The bus barely jiggled on Denver's smooth streets.

Do you really want to talk about this?

I did. I wanted to know everything that had happened to him, I wanted to see those ghost-days of his past in front of me, before my eyes, I wanted to know if the ghosts really did any haunting or if they were just ghosts for lack of an alternative.

I really did want to talk about that subject. Lots of people didn't, they thought it was best kept out of the official history, but sometimes questions gnaw at you like insects. And they really do gnaw, patient little silverfish scuttling between letters, numbers and stamps in the guerrilla files kept secret by the Armed Forces. Where was the missing son, and under what circumstances had he disappeared? Where was his cadaver buried, and how had his healthy body become a cadaver?

Were there no rights against the homeland? As time passed, the parents of those who went missing on the Araguaia also died, one by one. They died one by one without ever knowing what had happened to their guerrilla son, to their guerrilla daughter.

But as the commanders of the Armed Forces told their subordinates during the repression of the guerrilla movement, the orders were to watch, listen and stay quiet.

Ideally, the guerrillas should disappear, an old widow forgotten in her room. Closed windows, closed door, a tiny, frail heart beating behind flaccid muscles, drooping breasts, wrinkled skin. She had been nothing, didn't represent anything, what use was there in rubbing salt into the wound? The military group Terrorism Never Again would come to define it as:

A truly small residual group's adventure.

An illegal, underground party's deranged, incoherent idea to start a people's war without the support of the people, in order to impose socialism on them.

A Quixotic group's actions, further jeopardizing themselves, lost in the jungle and in the tangle of their own errors.

A few decades later, in the south of Pará, where Fernando used to live, there is no more forest. Back when it was still there, Brazil's official history was called the "Brazilian Miracle".

One of the most sensational things of all, in those days, was the Brazilian National Team's recent victory in the FIFA World Cup, in which it had become world champion for the third time. Oh, the 1970 World Cup! It was a team that had Pelé, Gérson, Jairzinho, Tostão, Rivelino, and Carlos Alberto Torres as captain. A team that has never been rivaled anywhere at any point in history. After missing out in England in 1966, why not raise the Jules Rimet Cup in all its glittering gold in Mexico's Azteca Stadium? Why not? Even if some clairvoyant supporter had known that the cup would be stolen and melted down years later, it wouldn't have diminished Brazil's excitement over the victory in the slightest.

Which ran parallel to other national sentiments. My history teacher may have explained this on one of those days when I was watching the pigeons outside, the dirty pigeons of Copacabana and their cooing and occasional deformed feet. But it was Fernando who summed it up for me, as the bus barely jiggled on Denver's smooth streets. The economic policy of the dictatorship brought down inflation and unemployment, and the country grew. (It would all get out of hand when an oil crisis came along to put a dampener on things. In the year of the military coup, Brazil's foreign debt was little more than three billion dollars. By the end of the military dictatorship, in 1985, when General Figueiredo asked everyone to forget him, it was over ninety billion.) At the same time, the country was told that the cake had to rise first before everyone could have a piece. And that was how minimum wages plummeted mid-Miracle. And the poorest members of the population became even poorer. In the mid-1970s, more than half of the Brazilian population was under- or malnourished.

I came to the conclusion that the saint who had worked the miracle had worn a wire halo covered with gold paper, like the ones we had once made for a Christmas play at school. The miracle-working saint levitated standing on a plank and when he tried to strike up a conversation with the plants and animals, the plants and animals didn't understand a thing.

During Operation Fish I, the residents of São João do Araguaia talked to the army about a *group of people from São Paulo* who were living in Faveira.

The investigators wore plain clothes and were under orders to keep that first phase of the operation absolutely secret. They left with a few names, a few suspects and a few certainties.

One of the certainties was that the enemy was better equipped for confrontation than they had thought, and that reinforcements were required.

Operation Fish II would come next. To watch, investigate, arrest, interrogate.

They conducted searches in Faveira and seized ammunition and a boat. They staked out a point on the Trans-Amazonian Highway where they thought they might surprise a certain suspect by the name of Joca. Who had bought land in Faveira and started receiving people whom he introduced to the locals as members of his family: a certain Dona Maria, a certain Cid, a certain Mário, a certain Luiz. A man of Japanese descent, a blonde woman. A couple called Beto and Regina.

This Joca had a large, diverse family, as they had discovered in Operation Fish I.

The military considered the hypothesis that they were inoffensive hippies, disenchanted with urban life, only to quickly discard it. They suspected that Joca was an experienced guerrilla from the National Liberation Action by the name of João Alberto Capiberibe.

And it was indeed him. But they never imagined that Dona Maria was Elza Monerat, a veteran communist who was almost sixty years old. Or that Mário and Cid were Maurício Grabois and João Amazonas, of the Brazilian Communist Party's central committee and former federal deputies.

The agents on the Trans-Amazonian Highway stakeout waited for Joca to appear. He no longer lived in Faveira, but according to locals he visited once a month, took care of whatever he needed to and then returned to an unknown place in the middle of the forest (*The forest is our second mother!*), passing along the Trans-Amazonian.

The agents waited for five days. In vain. You see, information also traveled in the opposite direction.

Manuela's letter to Chico, a piece of paper that later took up residence in the wooden El Coto de Rioja wine crate, at the back of a wardrobe in a suburb of Denver, was written before all this.

Manuela was bedridden with malaria and thought she was going to die. She ached all over, from head to foot. She vomited. Shook with fever. Other comrades had already been through it and worse things and were still there, but she felt so bad that she didn't think she'd make it. The suffering in her own body seemed more complex and specific than in other people's bodies.

In those parts it was common for people to die of malaria, yellow fever, leishmaniasis. Comrade Regina, who had been in Faveira a year earlier, had had brucellosis, anemia, fallen pregnant by her boyfriend Beto, and had an abortion as per the Party's orientation. The abortion wasn't carried out properly and she was finally granted leave to go get treatment elsewhere.

The fetus was still in her belly. She never returned.

Chico was working in the forest when bedridden Manuela thought she was going to die. He had been away for over a week.

You're not going to die, said Comrade Inês.

But her body no longer seemed to have the will to live. In her letter to Chico, Manuela wrote, with revolutionary flair: I admire you so much. Your strength, your ability. If I don't make it, please find a way to notify my parents in Rio de Janeiro. Tell them that I never regretted coming here. Dying sick in a bed isn't the same as dying in a war against the enemies of the people, it is true, but even so I don't regret it. I also want to say that I really like you. I wish life were different. You know. Really different. Completely different.

Chico knew. When he returned from the forest and read the letter from Manuela, who was burning up with fever but recovered from the malaria and recovered again all the times she got sick, he already knew.

You might be willing to lay down your life for the Party and its ideals (you have to in order to be a part of the Guerrilla Forces, otherwise when you realize you aren't it's too late). But to lay down love, not necessarily.

The woodsman who had studied in China, maker of weapons, a communist since he was a teenager, the man with a boy's face and firm arms who wasn't afraid of anything, who even before going to the Araguaia had been unable to get a job anywhere because of his sullied record (against the homeland there are no rights), thought it was possible to have both. The Araguaia Guerrilla Forces and the girl who went by the codename Manuela, who thought she was going to die of malaria.

Come on, Manuela. You're going to be fine.

A week later she was teaching again in the school created and run by the guerrillas, for children who had nothing, who only had what their families were able to take from the benevolence of the land and the rivers, the children of the squatters who feared the land-grabbers who were on the side of the power.

Brazil only remembered that infinite no man's land when the no man's land became a question of national security, in that era when Trans-Amazonian Highways came into being. But it wouldn't solve its problems, not even in the next half-century.

One of the things that Manuela couldn't have known when she was teaching those children was that in the future Bico do Papagaio would continue to be a poor region, abandoned by the government, and would be the setting for violent conflicts sparked by the coexistence of farmers, loggers, landless workers, prospectors, Indians, slave workers, gunmen and drug traffickers.

Years later, a police chief by the name of Hitler Mussolini would frequent the region, trying to deport Dominican friars fighting for the rights of local rural workers.

In that future, police officers would hold second jobs as security guards on big farms. Slave workers would labor under the watch of armed men and would sleep locked up in sheds. One adolescent girl rescued by investigators had no idea that she could be paid for her work. It hadn't occurred to her. She was fourteen years old and had been working since she was five.

The Party didn't want the guerrillas to have amorous dallyings. But what if they weren't dallyings? Some comrades appeared to be celibate. Others were married. And others were indeed in relationships that had been born there, in the middle of the forest, as they practised shooting or first aid.

So, one day when Manuela went to cut wood in the forest, Chico went with her. To help.

Como é que você se chama? Quando é que você me ama? Onde é que eu vou lhe falar? Como é que você não me diz quando é que você me faz feliz? Onde é que vamos morar? (What is your name? When will you love me? Where will I talk to you? Why won't you tell me when you are going to make me happy? Where are we going to live?)

Chico wasn't going to sing the song, tone-deaf as he was, but he could think it, since thoughts don't go off-key.

He could think it as he thought about Manuela. As he caught Manuela in a hug. Come here, girl. And she laughed. I thought I was going to die. How silly. (Who said "how silly", him or her?) I really like you too. (This was definitely him.)

That dense forest that blocked everything, that even blocked the sunlight. Once Chico dreamed that he was entering the forest and it was pitch-black. He couldn't see a thing. In the middle of the day. But *the forest is our second mother!* And in the middle of the forest you can hug and kiss someone you like, someone you think you really like, a lot, and sing songs mentally so as not to run the risk of going off-key. And later you can even sing a few lines of the song out loud, despite your voice and tone deafness. Just a few lines. Remove your clothes and reveal a body that is weak and strong at the same time. Ugly and beautiful. Very thin. Times two. A lot of insect bites. Calluses. Scars. Warmth, desire. All of it. Then put your clothes back on, hoist the firewood onto your back and take it to where it needs to be taken. As if it were weapons. As if it were a wounded companion.

One day I discovered a poem called "The Fish". It was pretty difficult. It was in one of those (pretty difficult) anthologies of American poetry that the librarian gave me to read, full of literary honesty and belief in the future. And which I read thinking that it was all going to be transferred to my brain, lodge there and make me a different person (better, if possible: I worked hard at it and had a sponsor), just as the TV had taught me other basic survival techniques.

A few years later, having reread the poem called "The Fish" many more times, the axis of my feelings shifting a little more with each reading, I decided it was my favorite. My Poem. Of all of the ones I'd sweated over in the pages of the anthologies in Denver Public Library.

I discovered that the author, Marianne, was the daughter of an engineer-inventor by the fine name of John Milton Moore (I'd like to be called John Milton Moore if I were a man. Evangelina Moore doesn't work, but Marianne Moore does. That is the name of the author of my favorite poem and it is a lovely name). Her father was committed to an institution for the mentally ill before she was born. I didn't find anything about her mother; she was just John's wife and was named, quite appropriately, Mary. Marianne liked boxing and baseball.

When I read the "The Fish", I was transported to a world of colors, of primordial movements. It contained crabs like green lilies and submarine toadstools.

And a turquoise sea of bodies. And crow-blue shells.

And a "sun split like spun" that was nice to repeat over and over, bringing with it an image of submerged shards of sunlight, shafts of sunlight. SUN SPLIT LIKE SPUN SUN SPLIT LIKE SPUN SUN SPLIT LIKE SPUN. Sun split like spun glass.

It had nothing to do with the studies by scientists at the University of Edinburgh revealing that fish can feel pain [citation required]. Not least because it was written well before them.

It also had nothing to do with the operations conducted by the Brazilian Armed Forces on the banks of the Araguaia River.

Those were other fish. The woman who wrote "The Fish" was dying when the Armed Forces trailed their dragnets for subversives through the Brazilian Amazon. And she had nothing to do with it. Just as no fish had anything to do with it. The story that was unraveling on the banks of the Araguaia was a human story. The fish only lent it their name.

Involuntarily, I might add – like confiscated savings accounts.

May I pet your dog?

I LIKED THE expression "smooth sailing" the first time I came across it. I tried to find the best translation in Portuguese but nothing was quite right. It meant easy progress. But the expression itself evoked boats, the sea and calm surfaces and took me back to the time when that made immediate sense.

"Smooth" was the satiny quality of the water, "sailing" was the verb for the sail that puffed out with the wind and crossed entire oceans.

The moment the English teacher at school congratulated me on my efforts and summed it all up in that "smooth sailing", I clearly saw myself in a sailboat making the tiniest tear in a perfectly silken sea, a progressive boat, a boat as pure and optimistic as the shoals of fish swimming beneath it.

I left school along liquid corridors, and the concrete of the side-walk was liquid.

So I sailed. In a single expression the English teacher had defined my first few weeks in an entirely landlocked state, without any contact with any beach or any ocean.

In terms of water, in Colorado, I had seen the reservoirs where people sailed around in circles on Sundays. Cascading rivers in the folds of the mountains, on which people practiced turbulent sports – navigating downstream in yellow boats that looked like giant kitchen sponges or in pointy kayaks. I never suspected that all that water would grow thin and lock itself away in ice in the months to come, storing its liquidity in the slow metabolism of hibernation.

But I sailed on calm seas, that is, I made easy progress, that is, I was being successful in my daily attempts to not trip up.

Boats that sail on calm seas know no gravel, no loose stones in their path, they know no feet. Their mobility is made of waves and wind. With the right waves and the right wind the sailboat slips along free of metaphysics. Like a first-grade equation.

Daniel, my father's name, was a valid name in several languages, I discovered to my delight. Daniel was Daniel in English, Portuguese and Spanish, the three languages I had contact with every day, there in Lakewood.

The plump man in the blue shirt and tie in the Jehovah's Witnesses pamphlet would no doubt be able to explain the biblical origins of the name. All I knew was that it had belonged to some-one who at some stage had had something to do with lions, accord-ing to legend. I didn't even know if he had fought them and won, with some intrinsically spiritual moral to be learned, or lost, with some intrinsically spiritual moral to be learned.

I suspected that Daniel didn't suspect that he had a

thirteen-year-old daughter named Vanja, who was a citizen of two countries and lived in harmonious linguistic chaos, a daughter who spoke English at school, Portuguese at home and Spanish with the neighbors.

And I sensed that I needed to maintain that smooth sailing towards Daniel. Life needed to become an orderly series of tasks. More or less like a sailor's day-to-day life must be. An orderly physical world full of calculations and angles that is needed for a boat to sail.

The same orderly physical world where hungry lions kill Daniel, where disinterested lions spare Daniel – it's hard to say. There are the between-the-lines in all stories. Some gods like bloody martyrs (in the style of Tim Treadwell and his bears in Alaska), others don't really care.

But at any rate I suspected that Daniel didn't suspect that I existed.

After a few phone calls, Fernando had finally located some people. Among them, that old friend of my mother's who lived in Santa Fé. But couldn't Daniel have been located with a telephone book too? He could have, if there weren't lots of Daniels with the same surname all over New Mexico and if Daniel still lived in New Mexico and if he happened to be listed.

But maybe he had crossed the border and was now in Arizona or Texas or even Colorado, or in Mexico even, on the other side of an even more borderly border, or in British Columbia or Argentina (why not?), or virtually anywhere else in the world. Or maybe that specific Daniel no longer existed, and there were just his namesakes scattered across the globe, a one-man diaspora.

The old friend of my mother's who lived in Santa Fé taught piano and was called June. It had been over ten years since she'd last seen Daniel, as she explained to Fernando. She told him that he had moved to San Antonio, in Texas, and then they had lost touch. Emails, that kind of thing? She had tried, said Fernando. She had written to a few people, but hadn't heard back yet. We'd have to wait a little.

After a few moments of silence:

Why didn't you ever ask your mother where your father was?

Because I didn't need to know. Because I don't think she knew. Because I don't think she would have wanted to tell me. I don't know. Why did you and she stop talking?

Because we didn't have any reason to keep talking to each other.

Didn't you have anything to talk about? Didn't you care about each other anymore?

We didn't have anything to talk about. We didn't care about each other anymore. That must have been it.

He was chopping kale. I picked up a piece of kale that had fallen on the ground and put it back on the chopping board. And I dared to ask: Why did you have to leave Brazil?

The knife thudded against the chopping board as he chopped. Plac. Plac. Plac.

They were after me.

The police?

The army.

What had you done?

Some things.

Wrong things?

In their opinion, yes. Those were hard times.

I didn't know if I should shake Fernando to get him to spit out what he ended up telling me over the months to come, as ice covered the cascading rivers and the reservoirs, and afterwards, as the ice melted and swelled the cascading rivers and the reservoirs of the following summer. To get him to tell me about firearms and that other woman (Manuela/Joana) before London and my mother, before Lakewood, Colorado, and well before Vanja. The woman from the letter that lived in the seclusion of the wooden El Coto de Rioja wine crate.

But the idea of shaking Fernando was still sort of frightening. The idea of taking hold of those mounds of muscle and rattling them, as if I had any right to his life. I didn't. The fact that I was there just because he had once given me the gift of his name on my birth certificate was already a big deal.

When I think about Fernando today, nine years after those first few weeks in Lakewood, I remember his arms. That was where the real Fernando, his soul, his personality must have lived. The arms that were only a hypothetical force during his daily hours as a security guard at Denver Public Library, cat claws inside a cat's paws. The arms that I saw removing marks from windows and dust from surfaces and trash from other people's floors on so many occasions. The arms that had once tensed with the weight of a weapon – I don't know the weight of a weapon, I don't know the weight that you add to a weapon or subtract from it depending on the purpose with which it is picked up. The arms that I knew had wrapped around my mother's body, 360 degrees (love, a weapon, arms that disarm), and the body of that other woman before my mother and London and New Mexico and Colorado. The arms hard at work over a frying pan making *farofa* with the kale and the manioc flour bought in a store that sold Brazilian products. The arms that came home holding a red plastic sled when the first days of snow in early November held the promise of slippery slopes. The arms that pushed me down the slippery slopes while on the inside I was stiff, raw panic. The arms that learned to overcome their own inability to hug someone else's daughter in a goodnight ritual that in theory didn't even need to exist. The arms that closed the door after answering the Jehovah's Witness woman for the second and third time (had he read the pamphlet? Bible in hand, she wanted to know if he had any questions. And he didn't have the courage to say that the pamphlet had ended up in the trash, and he said he still hadn't had time to read it). The quiet arms that held my math book as the muscles in his face tensed with concentration.

We'd have to wait, as June from Santa Fé had said and as Fernando had repeated.

I didn't have any other commitment besides that one, to wait.

Five days a week I went to school. Two days a week I didn't. And meanwhile, I waited.

Five days a week I ate lunch at the same table as Aditi Ramagiri and her friends, in the school cafeteria, and one lusterless Wednesday I looked differently at a boy called Nick during math class, and the lusterless Wednesday became the great Mogul, Shah Jahan's diamond, said to be missing since the seventeenth century and which I had just found, somewhat awkwardly.

I would have to wait.

One day, as I was passing a light-blue house on my way back from school, our Salvadorian neighbors' son was standing on the sidewalk. He was a short, stocky boy, with a funny face.

He said hi in Spanish. *Hola.*

I answered.

He asked *¿Como te llamas?*

Vanja, I said. *¿Y tu?*

Carlos.

Carlos wasn't an appropriate name for a child, I thought. Maybe all the Carloses in the world had been born adults. Except him, with his Ninja Turtles T-shirt and an American football in his little hands.

¿Juegas? I asked, pointing at the ball with my chin.

No, he said, simply.

Yo tampoco.

Two days later he knocked on Fernando's front door holding a book in English for children a lot younger than himself. Carlos's spoken English was very poor. And he could barely read at all. The book had a dozen phrases and huge drawings of cars, motorbikes, airplanes, buses, ambulances, fire engines and other motor vehicles that slid through the world with ease, grace and fossil fuels.

I asked how old he was.

Carlos looked at me with his chubby face, almond-shaped eyes behind glasses and short, spiky hair, and said nine. He handed me the book and asked if I could read it to him.

I offered him a glass of *guaraná*. From the store that sold Brazilian products.

We sat on the couch a palm's breadth apart. I began to read.

Carlos wanted to quickly skip to the next page to see the next picture.

I explained: Carlos, you have to pay attention, dude.

I started running my finger under the words as I read. Carlos began imitating them. A few minutes later, he perched his hand on my forearm and left it there, like a warm, slightly sweaty little bird. I wasn't sure if he really understood the words or if he was just pretending, if it was merely a strategy to keep me reading.

You shouldn't get too close to people, Fernando had told me. The Brazilian habit of hugging and kissing everyone. If you want to greet someone, shake their hand. That's how things work around here.

In Rio de Janeiro, people are always bumping into one another. You bump into people in supermarket aisles, in queues, on the sidewalk, in the bus, in the metro. You don't get out of the way when other people need to pass you. Other people don't get out of the way when you need to pass them. We go around saying excuse me and forging paths with our own bodies. *Licença*, we say, sometimes, and sometimes with so little effort that the word disappears into us and becomes an indistinct *ss-ss*. We are forever hugging and kissing people we have known for ten years and people we have just met and we say hi darling to everyone. We pat dogs that are being walked by their owners. At the very most, we ask does he/she bite? after verifying which pronoun to use by looking under the animal's legs for a pair of testicles or the lack thereof. If the owner says he/she doesn't bite, we plunge our fingers into his/her fur without asking permission, stroke his/her ears, tickle his/her belly. And it's nice, and the world is essentially made up of surfaces rubbing against one another and an exchange of heat.

Here you ask permission first if you want to pet someone's dog, Fernando told me the first time I saw two bubbly golden retrievers with fur that was better cared for than my hair and I threw myself at them and they corresponded with legitimate passion and the owner gave me a dirty look. Say: May I pet your dog? I repeated it mentally so I wouldn't forget it: May I pet your dog?

Carlos and I finished reading the book and I asked what he had liked the most and he said the ambulance. Then he asked for some more *guaraná*, a word that he pronounced perfectly. From that day on, Carlos became my afternoon companion. And I, his afternoon companion.

Carlos didn't have *papeles*. Neither did his mother. Or his father or sister. They had arrived in the United States as tourists, though they weren't tourists, a little more than a year earlier. Their visas had expired and they hadn't returned to El Salvador.

Carlos's sister worked as a chambermaid in a hotel in the tech center. She said she was going to save money to study medicine at Harvard. When I move to Massachusetts, she would say, I'm going to room with someone from med school and I'm going to have a red couch in my apartment.

Carlos's father worked as a waiter in a Mexican restaurant.

Carlos's mother didn't work. One day Fernando told me that she couldn't work. That woman's unstable. Haven't you ever noticed? She has some kind of problem. I don't know what it is, but it must be something serious. That woman's unstable.

I thought he was joking. He wasn't.

I find an open question in Yahoo. What can we brazilians do to end this latin invasion of brazil especially são paulo?

And another question: what do you guys think of all the bolivians who've been flocking to são paulo recently? many of them don't have visas and take jobs that should go to unemployed brazilians, and our slack government doesn't do a thing.

Someone replies: Bolivians are no less, no more human than you. If they want to work, God bless whomever gives them a job.

Someone replies: Unfortunately, Brazil has always been a refuge for every kind of crook, ever since the days of the empire. And nothing has changed. Government? What's a government for again?!!!!!!!!!!!!!!! Hahaha.

Someone replies: There really are a lot of them. Until a few years ago, they say there were 50,000 Bolivians in SP, but by last year the number had grown to almost 300,000!!!!!!! (99.9% illegal). And that was just in the city of SP – imagine how many there are in the whole of Brazil . . . My cousin lives in Belenzinho – if you walk down the street on the weekend, you don't see a single Brazilian, just Bolivians, and there are more every day! I'm not against immigrants, but the growth of the Bolivian population in SP is scary!

Someone replies: Brazil's always been "the world's trash can". Nothing is controlled here and the Bolivians know it. If it were a European country, they'd be afraid to walk down the street and get caught in a "razzia".

Someone replies: There are illegal immigrants all over the world my friend. What about the millions of illegal Brazilians in the US, who even commit petty crimes? He who lives in a glass house shouldn't throw stones!

Another question. Why did German immigrants chose Brazil as their destination?

Someone replies: Because in the days when they started emigrating to Brazil our country was the one that offered the most support for those who wanted to work and move up in life, and besides, the German's aren't stupid, they know our country is one of the best in the world

Someone replies: Easy to get in and mulattas dancing samba in bikinis.

Carlos didn't have permission to use the computer at his house and came over almost every day after school to ask me if he could play on ours. Only after you've done your homework, I said the first time he asked. And if Fernando says it's OK. It's his computer, not mine.

Carlos went home. But as soon as the Saab pulled up at the curb he came and rang the doorbell again, holding up his homework to show me that he'd done almost everything and that he'd only left one thing blank – could I help him with it? What's the difference between its and it's? And then could he play on the computer?

Until one morning the thermometer showed 43 degrees Fahrenheit. The day before it had been 86. I opened the door to a strange, gray, two-dimensional sky. A brown rabbit was peering at me from the straggly strip of grass, not sure if it should flee or not. Staring out the side of its head, like all of the other creatures for whom the world offers itself in double, one for each eye, and whose attention is always split schizophrenically. The rabbit sat there chewing the grass with its whiskers bobbing up and down, in its little tuft of existence, uncertain as to the potential threat I posed, which it assessed with its left eye.

I got a jacket, suspicious of that revolution of temperatures. Unsure if it was for real. At school, as I waited for class to start, I drew a diamond on my jeans with a pen. The great multifaceted Mogul, the King of the World's enormous diamond.

Nick passed me and said hey and I answered hey without looking up to feign disinterest. Later he asked me for my pen and asked if he could draw something on my jeans too, OK, I said, and he drew four letters, NICK, and told me he was an eco-anarchist.

That was the day the season changed officially, said the teachers.

I thought it was curious. Watching the seasons change was a little luxury. Like playing cricket or going to Greece. The trees all decided that, being autumn, they had to do something. Turn yellow, for example, or start dropping leaves on the ground. And the streets would become thick carpets between street sweeper visits over the following weeks, the re-offending leaves challenging passersby. Old things, or more than old, dead things, the disincarnated leftovers of summer. Leaves that would engender critters underneath them. Actually, they wouldn't, because the dryness of the place hardly allowed any critters to come into being in this manner; they had to be pretty tough there. One day I saw a man ride his bicycle through the leaves, churning up a small rustling, fire-colored wake behind him.

In Rio de Janeiro I had seen almond trees changing color. But there were no almond trees in Lakewood, Colorado. I saw aspens and read in the dictionary that the translation was *faia preta* or *choupo* or *álamo*. I thought it was strange that it could have three names in Portuguese. The maple had only one: *bordo*. And Fernando didn't know the names of the other trees – not even the one that would soon be red all over, like a flaming torch wedged into the sidewalk.

When we went on an autumn outing – an expedition to the corn maze – the radio station was holding a fundraising campaign. Show your support by calling such-and-such a number and making your donation NOW. Keep the public radio on the air.

A woman with a husky voice identified herself and said she was a pianist and that she was there to declare her support and ask YOU to do as she had done, calling such-and-such a number and making your donation. Then the chocolatey-voiced announcer said he was going to play a track from the husky-voiced pianist's latest CD. And he reminded listeners: if you appreciate this music, if you want to keep it alive, call such-and-such a number and make your donation now. Then the husky-voiced woman came on playing the piano, accompanied by drums and a double bass. The piano, like the pianist, seemed a little husky too, and it was nice to listen to it/her as I snuggled into myself and my jacket, in the front seat of the car.

Fernando was wearing a short-sleeved T-shirt.

Aren't you cold?

No. You get used to it.

I turned to the back seat. Carlos seemed like a miniature person, not a child, but a miniature person, under the seatbelt. His eyes, enlarged by his thick glasses, shone, and he said, almost shouting: *¡Yo entiendo un poco el portugués!*

Fernando had a cleaning job to do and Carlos and I were going along too on the condition that we wouldn't get in the way, and Fernando would take us to the corn maze afterwards.

Another thing that happens when you have been away from home for too long is that you learn about new things in the new place via the new language and soon the tongue you speak is a strange combination of your native syntax and a two-faceted vocabulary. I didn't say *labirinto no milharal*, in Portuguese. I said "corn maze". When I knocked on Carlos's door and invited him to come with us he said yay, *qué bueno*, corn maze, and ran off to ask his mother. As if she wouldn't let him.

Aditi Ramagiri, my friend with the Indian face and name who had been born in Columbus, Ohio, who a short time later would become one of the school's biggest pot-heads and a prolific producer of weed cookies, said she wouldn't be able to invite me to her birthday party because her mother only let her invite people who had already been to her house at least five times or whose house she had already been to at least five times. The party was that Saturday. I envisaged Veronica Crump and Leslie Yang and Jessica Martinez and Betty Tajul-Amar at Aditi's birthday party, all of them eligible under Mrs. Ramagiri's five-times rule.

I mentioned it to Fernando at lunch, between mouthfuls of the couscous that came in a yellow box and was ready in five minutes.

He grumbled something with his mouth full, in English, that I didn't understand. And said he was going to take me to the corn maze and that it would be much better than what's-her-name-that's-right-Aditi-Ramagiri's damned party.

I wanted to say that it wasn't Aditi's fault. I wasn't mad at her. I wasn't even mad at Mrs. Ramagiri, customs are customs, rules are rules, each family has its own, and Fernando grumbled something else with his mouth full, in English, that I didn't understand.

In the back seat, as the husky-voiced woman's husky piano played between bursts of fundraising, and Fernando drove the red Saab towards the corn maze, Carlos sucked on his juice box a little more and said: More *portugués, por favor.*

I was the one who got us out of the corn maze. Fernando left it all up to me. Carlos was nervous, with the nervousness of all young children about to see the Big Bad Wolf try to trick Little Red Riding Hood for the billionth time. What big eyes you have, etc. The drama is there even when they know the ending off by heart. And they suffer just the same. And in this manner children test the world, make sure that it really will answer the same question the same way every time. And they conclude that it will. Yet another false campaign promise of the adult world. Yes, Carlos, we are coherent. Grow up and see for yourself.

Carlos walked down the corridors of the maze hewn in the corn field as if he could really get lost there, and for all time. He held my hand. And looked into my eyes from time to time, as if checking to see how reliable I was.

I did what he expected of me: I pretended that the danger was real and on our heels, death waving at us in a corn field in a suburb of Denver sponsored by Starbucks, the First Bank of Colorado and Spicy Pickle. As if we were in a Stephen King novel or a film adaptation of a Stephen King novel.

The afternoon fell and the temperature was dropping and now even Fernando had resorted to a jacket. Carlos's cheeks were red. So it really was true that climatic revolutions annihilated the broad, horizontal heat of July, of August. It really was true that September came and at the end of that month it was autumn and with autumn things changed interests, like lovers who were already a bit bored of one another.

Fernando was always looking at some place that seemed strange and faraway. Fernando seemed strange and faraway. But that was him in general.

Later, back at home, Fernando spread out a dog-eared map of New Mexico and a dog-eared map of Colorado on the dining table. He joined them at the border. They were so worn that their folds were faded and had already torn in some places. He showed me where Albuquerque was. He explained the distances, traced the highways with his fingers. He talked about the winter I was born. He didn't like Interstate 25 but it was the quickest route to Albuquerque. The prettiest was the Interstate 285, which left the southeastern tip of Denver's urban cluster and wound its way into the mountains. I read the names of the cities it passed through. Fairplay, Poncha Springs, Saguache, Monte Vista, Alamosa, Antonito. And in New Mexico, Tres Piedras, Ojo Caliente, and the capital, Santa Fé.

I wasn't used to maps, but there was something intriguing about them. Sitting there, in Fernando's living room, at night, a mapable world didn't seem possible. It was all an abstraction – different highways, borders, states and countries, towns with names like Ojo Caliente or Fairplay. But those abstractions were really there, situated in very specific, localizable places, hence maps, and that was the intriguing part. If I got in a car and followed those tiny yellow veins and continued following the tiny yellow veins portrayed by other maps I would come across different borders, states and countries, towns with names like Fairplay and Ojo Caliente, and Juárez if I continued, and Chihuahua and Zacatecas. And if I carried on, overland, I would pass through Mexico City and Oaxaca, and then there would be Guatemala City and Tegucigalpa, Managua, Alajuela, Panama City, Medellín, Bogotá, and suddenly I would see Amazonian Brazil before me. Continuing, there would be the Araguaia and its memory and its forgetting of a guerrilla army, and from there, crossing another three states, I would arrive once again at Copacabana Beach and its Atlantic mollusks dreaming blue dreams at the bottom of the sea.

In all of these places, all of them, there were many Daniels and many fathers of thirteen-year-old girls. Some had possibly even gone astray.

I'd like to go to New Mexico, I said, without even realizing I'd spoken, which is why I was surprised when Fernando shrugged and said we can go.

Can we visit the house I used to live in? (The house I used to live in: a character in a fairytale. An imaginary being.) Can we visit this June lady?

Why not?

I looked at him and in my throat I asked, without letting my voice out: Why are you doing all this?

Mentally, he answered: Because you asked me to.

Then I looked away. Neither of us was very fond of sentimental words, even sentimental words that weren't actually spoken, that laid in wait. The mere potential, the simple possibility that something of the sort might exist threatened to make the world mushy and sappy, and in a mushy, sappy world people don't live, they just slip about and complain.

Man's wolf

MY FATHER. THE idea still sounded almost fanciful. A treasure hunt. A pot of gold at the end of a rainbow. What if I made it to the end of the rainbow and the pot of gold was really filled with second-rate chocolate coins, the sort that taste like wax? What if the rainbow had no end?

Perhaps my father was an optical phenomenon too. Red, orange, yellow, green, blue, indigo, violet. The dispersion of sunlight. The "X" that marked the location of the treasure on the map but which was maybe a silent hole that someone had beat me to. A joke. A hoax.

My father might be: in prison, dead, traveling, exiled, in a hospital or mental institution, living on the streets, on an island in the Caribbean, on a military base in Bulgaria, on a scientific base in Antarctica, in a Buddhist monastery in the Philippines, looking at paintings and smoking a pipe on a bridge in Paris.

My father might be too old, too young, weird, too good-looking, too thin, brilliant, aloof, bald, good-humored, too fat, extroverted, religious, hairy, ugly, very learned, short-sighted, athletic, kind of quarrelsome, bearded, successful, very musically talented. My father might have fathered other daughters and other sons.

I mentally listed off the possibilities as I made coffee, certain that my father would allow himself to be divined in any of them. It made me a little anxious. Anxiety is a hostile feeling that grips your stomach with crooked, cold, possessive fingers.

The coffee, a Brazilian brand bought in the store that sold Brazilian products, dripped into the pot. The toast toasted in the toaster. The house, snuggled up in drawn curtains and closed doors, smelled of coffee and toast.

Fernando was asleep and perhaps my father's faces, or my mother's face, were in his dreams. Or the faces of that Amazonian war which, I had yet to find out, he would never forget. He would forget his phone number, his address, his own name, and the sound of his own voice before he would forget that. When the enemy advances, you withdraw, and when you have to withdraw sometimes you stumble.

He was asleep and I was making the coffee that would sit there in the artificial heat of the electric coffee-maker for too long until all of its integrity was suffocated in the taste of burnt straw. I drank the coffee fresh and ate my toast and got my backpack and jacket.

In late October Carlos and I went trick-or-treating in the neighborhood wearing black capes and masks with bulging eyes and devilish expressions. When I got home, Fernando was sitting in the living room in the dark, hands crossed behind his head. He was listening to an old Brazilian song from before I was born and perhaps before he was born, which I recognized because my mother used to listen to it too.

Who's that?

Noel Rosa, he replied.

Hmm.

I sat next to him. I reached into the bag of candies and picked one at random.

Want one? I asked.

He said yes. I picked something else at random and we sat there in the dark eating sickly-sweet candies with artificial fruit flavorings, as I thought about the song that my mother also used to listen to and he thought some thoughts all of his own.

Suddenly I looked at him and thought that his wrinkles, even in the weak light coming from outside, were all deeper, more pronounced, and that the skin of his face was like wet clothes hanging on a coat hanger.

I touched my own face with both hands. I ran my fingertips around my eyes, across my forehead.

At what moment did you realize that you were starting to age? Was there already some kind of sign at the age of thirteen, a miniscule wrinkle, a tiny valley beginning to be eroded where previously there had only been a plain? There was a fine fuzz above my upper lip. I had to start removing it. My mother used to use a hair removal cream and would have a white moustache for eight minutes, once a month. Then she would wash it off and the area would be a bit red for a few hours. The cream had a strange smell, a mixture of floral essence and science lab.

When's your birthday, Fernando? I asked.

Today, he said.

What?

Today, October 31.

Seriously? Halloween?

I wondered if that was why the lines in his face were deeper – because it was his birthday. Maybe these things didn't happen progressively but in waves, in cycles, and when it was your birthday your body realized it had to keep pace with the number indicative of your age, give or take a year. As if it was suddenly woken by an alarm clock and, still groggy, with heavy eyes, went off to go about the business of aging. To then lie down again and wait until it was time to age a little more.

The next day I invited Carlos to go with me to look for a present for Fernando. We bought a yellow T-shirt that didn't look like anything Fernando would wear. But he wore it that very same day, and took Carlos and me out for pizza and Carlos and I drank ginger ale and he had a Mexican beer in a glass mug with a wedge of lemon on the edge. He took the lemon and squeezed it into the beer and then left it bobbing there, which I found a little repugnant, because it made me think of refuse, trash cans and stinky organic leftovers.

Fernando looked like an extraterrestrial in the yellow T-shirt and I think he knew it, but he wore it with conviction that day and on several other occasions. Every time Carlos saw him in the yellow T-shirt he'd say: *La camisa de cumpleaños*. And Fernando would pat his head, and he would then smooth down his hair, as if it was possible to mess up his eternal crew cut. Carlos was visibly pleased by that moment of male camaraderie, comments about the shirt, pats on the head that were a variation of pats on the back, adapted to their height and age difference. The yellow made Fernando look one hundred percent wrong, and that didn't bother him, or me, or Carlos.

During the birthday pizza, Carlos wanted to know how old Fernando had turned. Fifty-seven, said Fernando.

You old, said Carlos. How say old in *portugués*?

Velho, said Fernando.

Velho, said Carlos imitating him, laughing. He thought the word was funny. *Velho*, he repeated. And he apparently liked the idea of Fernando being old. He reached across the table with his fat little hand and placed it on Fernando's. I like you *así mismo*. I not care you are *velho*. *Eres mi amigo*. My friend. How say friend in *portugués*?

Amigo, I said.

Ah! He was pure happiness. He was always pure happiness when he discovered words that were the same in his language and ours. When he came across yet another of our many Latin intersections. *Amigo en portugués, amigo en español. Qué bueno.*

He was wearing a red sweatshirt that was a little too small for him, with a baseball on it. Carlos was forever surrounded by the balls of sports he didn't play.

Chico and Manuela were living together when the war began in April of 1972. By this time they had already been transferred from Faveira to the Chega com Jeito base.

For Pedro, the first guerrilla captured, the war was something completely different and had begun earlier. When he tried to kill himself in his cell he didn't slash his wrists: he had learned in his training that it rarely killed anyone. Instead, he made deep cuts in the veins near his elbows, using razors which had ended up in his hands he didn't know how.

He survived (fascists!) and was tied to the bed. But in the forest he used the legitimate perturbation resulting from his condition (*Now you're going to experience the torture methods we learned in Vietnam*, an officer told him) to disorient the agents of repression: tripping, glassy eyes. He had been taken back to the Araguaia to recognize the guerrilla training sites. In the home of his godchild's parents, who lived in the region, the officers confirmed: you're a liar! How can you christen a child if you're a communist and communists don't believe in God? In prison in Xambioá (which wasn't the beautiful Xangri-La in the middle of a Himalayan valley), in a cell without a toilet, he heard a woman's screams that seemed to be coming from a torture session. Bluffing, they told him they were the screams of Tereza, his wife. Pedro was given electric shocks in the cuts in his arms. On one occasion they held a knife to his eye and said repeat that you are a communist. He was strung up from the ceiling naked. He kept on surviving. After all, as a clergyman had once said, you don't get confessions with bonbons.

In the outside world, the war began and Fernando was in the war. The same Fernando who would one day spread out a dog-eared map of New Mexico and a dog-eared map of Colorado in front of me on the dining table. So much time, so many lives woven into time; is man man's wolf?

I look at my arms without scars and think about cuts and

electric shocks. And I wonder how lives turned inside out and people turned inside out find their right-way-out again.

They don't. They become cousins of the tree that was born on a steep slope, its trunk forever crooked and its leaves growing towards the sun, believing, because that's what leaves do. They become cousins of the stray dog that eats the food that someone gives it one day because that's what dogs do. In Lakewood, Colorado, there were no stray dogs. In Copacabana there were and they were almost always ugly and always did everything with urgency; they urgently lived that life that was limited to urgently living that life without pet shops. If you set a plate of food on the ground and made it obvious that you weren't going to kick them if they approached, the strays of Copacabana would come, but they wouldn't eat. They would devour. In seconds. Whatever the food and whatever the amount. Is man also the wolf's wolf? The dog's wolf? When the army invaded the Chega com Jeito base and news reached the Gameleira base, one of the first things they did in their retreat was to kill the camp dog so it wouldn't attract the soldiers' attention with its barking.

The war started for Fernando, who was Chico in that place on that day. Fish III was the name given to the anti-guerrilla operation, whose aim was *to conduct an armed invasion of the "TARGET" in order to capture, neutralize and/or destroy the enemy* (the "TARGET" being a particular region where they suspected that there were subversive elements).

Fernando told me that the guerrillas fled. It was a narrow escape. From the forest, they actually saw the army surrounding the main house, helicopter and everything.

In the following days, the army found other bases, further south. They didn't catch anyone there either, but they seized homemade bombs, ammunition, food, medicine, a sewing machine, clothes, backpacks. As well as, of course, subversive literature. The army moved with difficulty through the forest. The only helicopter they had at the time was out on loan.

They were suspicious of a man moving a little too fast along a trail one morning. They stopped him and asked for explanations, the explanations weren't enough and the man, who was really the guerrilla Geraldo, was arrested, beaten, held underwater and forced to stand on open cans. On his person they found a note that said *C: army in the area. cmdr. B.* He was doomed. In Brasilia, a few days later, they found out that Geraldo was really José Genoino Neto, a communist who had been underground for four years. For three of which he had been living there, on the Araguaia, preparing the guerrilla forces.

The military was preparing "Civic-Social Actions," to mask the real reasons for its presence there and to try to win over the population, in a tug-of-war with the social work carried out by the communists. With Operation Fish IV, in May, the military intended to correct the mistakes of past operations and obtain more information on the enemy's identity, numbers and location. Officers from the army, navy and air force and the Pará military police were given the task of infiltrating the population.

That month the first military officer was killed by the Araguaia guerrillas: twenty-six-year-old Corporal Odílio Rosa. With a bullet in his groin, in a surprise brook-side encounter, when everything seemed calm and the forest was almost pleasant, almost comfortable, set against a naïve symphony of insects and birds with no political leanings.

On one side, four army officers and the woodsman who was accompanying them. On the other, two communist guerrillas. In that first confrontation, the guerrillas Osvaldão and Simão fired two shots. One hit Sergeant Morais and the other killed Corporal Rosa, whose body was left in the forest for a week before it was retrieved.

The surprise factor and numerical advantage, according to the Armed Forces, explained the defeat. The report also attributed the difficulty of removing Corporal Rosa's body to a supposed death threat made by the subversives to anyone who tried to retrieve it.

Along came Operation Fish V, whose mission was to retrieve the body.

The military decided on the ostensive deployment of troops in the region. This time they had observation planes and helicopters. Three platoons and a detachment of paratroopers headed for the Araguaia.

In that month of May the guerrillas also issued their first official announcement. It didn't mention the Party or the training that had been taking place in the forest for some years. But it announced the creation of the Union for Freedom and the Rights of the People, the ULDP.

The people united and armed will defeat their enemies.
Down with land grabbing!
Long live freedom!
Death to the military dictatorship!

For a free, independent Brazil!
Somewhere in the Amazon, May 25, 1972.
Commanders of the Araguaia Guerrilla Forces

Then Chico felt fear, for the first time. And he learned the art of mistrust.

He didn't know he had it in him. Maybe because he'd never looked death square in the face before, eye to eye. He had heard about it, heard descriptions of it, passed by it and perhaps even brushed past it unwittingly (scuse me, sorry) and kept walking, with the long strides and sunny whistle of the self-assured. Meanwhile, death, in a hat and overcoat, turned and frowned at that unconcerned individual's back. But to look straight at it and find its eyes wide open, undisguised, with the unspeakable inside them, to get through that unfair fight, now that was something else. For the first time he told Manuela that he didn't think the guerrillas would win.

They're too strong, said Chico.

Don't lose heart. They don't know their way around the forest. We've been here much longer. (Could it be that, of the two of them, she, who didn't have the Peking Military Academy under her belt, who didn't know how to make weapons, would be the one to tame her fear like a snake charmer, to walk over hot coals and sleep on a bed of nails?)

It doesn't matter, said Chico. They hire woodsmen. People sell themselves for next to nothing.

People sold themselves for next to nothing. The first guerrilla was killed not long afterwards, as a result of a tip-off from a peasant known as Cearensinho. Sent to his house to get a roll of tobacco, the guerrilla Jorge ran into the army and was machine-gunned down. Cearensinho had been considered a friend.

They're too strong, said Chico. By the end of May the army had more than two hundred men in the region. Not that Chico was up on the numbers.

By the end of May the army also had a list of five prisoners in a document entitled *Special information no. 1*. Among them, a boat man and farmer who was found hanged in his cell, a "known communist", a "lawyer" and another two men about whom nothing was said. It didn't mention the arrests of a further four inhabitants of the region or the capture of four guerrillas.

The ULDP (or "the terrorists of southeastern Pará") wrote a manifesto containing twenty-seven demands. Among them were: *Land for farming and legal titles. Reduction of taxes for rural labor and small businesses; tax exemption for small and medium-size farmers; an end to police participation in tax collection. Medical assistance in all districts, with itinerant clinics in boats and trucks. The creation of schools in villages, on the banks of the major rivers and near plantations; the building of boarding schools for children from distant locations. Protection for women; in the event of divorce, the right to part of the couple's estate and domestic possessions; pregnancy care; practical courses for the training of midwives. Work, schooling and physical education for young people; soccer and basketball fields, athletics tracks and recreation centers. Respect for all religious beliefs, with permission to practise all forms of shamanism and Spiritism. The employment of a good portion of taxes in the construction of highways, the paving of streets, the installation of electric and water facilities, the maintenance of schools and medical services. Plans for urbanization and development in cities and towns; aid for the building of homes; incentives for the creation of libraries and radio stations. Respect for the property of others, without harm to society; support for progressive private initiatives, small and medium-size factories and craftwork.*

Some time later, the army would use the Corporal Rosa Clearing as a symbolic place for the summary execution of guerrillas. And it was only more than three decades later that it was brought to light in the newspapers, when the army's former guides broke their silence during searches for the bones of the missing.

I read a comment online: Why don't they start using the Clearing again? But do the job properly this time. It's our only chance to live in a decent country.

I read another comment: The army did what it HAD TO DO GIVEN THE circumstances at the time. Speaking of which, it's time they did it again to take down the corrupt band of thieves who've taken over Brasilia!

I read another comment: Only cowards and criminals are afraid of the truth. It's definitely the case of those who are so opposed to shedding light on the facts about the executions on the Araguaia. Those cowards are obviously worried about having to explain themselves to their children, grandchildren and friends when they discover that the image of hero and protector of the Homeland that they had of them is false; they're really just a bunch of sadistic torturers.

I read another comment: What bugs me is paying money for these excavations. It should be paid for by the Brazilian Communist Party and cohorts who took the irresponsible from their homes, coaxed, indoctrinated, trained and made them into fanatics, then gave them weapons so they could play at being Che Guevara, all at the orders of the cruelest of dictators, Fidel Castro.

June called me last night, said Fernando. You were already in bed. She apparently knows someone who knows where Daniel's mother is.

Daniel's mother. An absolutely entirely new universe. While searching for my father, I had stumbled across a grandmother who was one hundred percent alive, material, tangible, with definite coordinates. And I hadn't the faintest idea what that meant. Suddenly my life began to fill with potential relatives. Could it be that I had a whole series of aunts, uncles, cousins, great aunts and uncles, second cousins? A family tree as happy as an oak, replete with branches and leaves and fruit? I'd never thought about it.

According to this person, Daniel's mother lives near Santa Fé. Her name is Florence and she's an artist.

An artist grandmother to boot. I mentally sketched a portrait of a very thin old hippie, with braids in her gray hair and a batik blouse.

Can you call her?

Well, to start with, June still hasn't got her phone number. But even if I did call her what would I say? Hi Daniel's mom, you don't know me, but I'm here with your son's teenage daughter. Could you by any chance tell me if he's alive and, if he is, where he is at the moment?

Outside was the noise of that weird contraption, that reverse vacuum cleaner that they used to clean the dry leaves from the streets, piling them up in compact little hills.

Sorry, said Fernando. But stop and think about it. What would you or I say on the telephone to Daniel's mother?

What do we do, then?

I'm not sure. I'll think about it. June offered to help. I have a cleaning job to go to. Wait for me for lunch, I won't be long.

He opened the door, looked out at the street and stopped for a moment. I wonder why there's a police car in front of Carlos's house?

The next day we found out that Carlos's sister, who worked as a chambermaid in a hotel in the tech center and intended to study medicine at Harvard, had quit her job and gone to Florida with her boyfriend.

What's she going to do there? I asked Fernando, after he had a brief chat with Carlos's dad. (Fernando never would have gone to Carlos's dad to ask about the whys and wherefores of the presence of the police car, or anything else, but they had run into one another in the street, and Carlos's dad had told him the story as if he were a political prisoner anxious to cooperate and avoid torture.)

I have no idea. He didn't say and I didn't ask. His wife was hysterical. The neighbor called the police. In a nutshell.

Did they arrest her?

He laughed. No, they didn't arrest her.

And, after a time, he added:

The neighbor shouldn't have stuck her nose in and called the police.

Are they going to send them back to their country?

Not that I know of, said Fernando.

That morning I studied math, finished reading a book and wrote the report I had to write, got in a mess with the facial hair removal cream and trimmed my hair a little in front of the mirror. Then I went to Carlos's house. He was sitting very quietly on the floor, in front of the TV.

Carlos, tu amiga Vanja, announced his dad's moustache. I didn't see his mother.

Carlos looked at me, still serious. It was the seriousness of children who are suddenly a little less children. Pokémons slid across the TV screen in the company of Japanese children with giant eyes and pointy hair.

Hola, he said. And he held out a packet of potato chips and asked if I wanted some.

I sat down in front of the Pokémons. Carlos slowly slid his fingers through the carpet and held my hand. Then he smiled when the Japanese boy with giant eyes shouted Pikachu, I choose you! and asked me if he could come over and play on Fernando's computer when the cartoon was over.

Outside, a rare heavy rain was impregnating the semiarid world with a strange element. And the moisture hung in the air: perplexity. A semicolon between two states: dry and very dry.

It's always strange when it rains in places like this. It feels like something has gone wrong, like some prior agreement has been violated. And then the rain moves on and its memory migrates into plump-leaved plants that flourish in another sense of the verb flourish.

Carlos's hysterical mother had no way of knowing, in fact, none of us did, that her golden future lay with her runaway daughter.

The ex-chambermaid from the hotel in Denver's tech center and ex-future Harvard student hadn't gone to Florida for nothing.

After spending several years serving watery coffee and bacon and eggs in a diner, she would say goodbye to her excessively jealous boyfriend and succumb to the routine attempts at seduction of a regular customer. Who frequented the establishment not for its watery coffee or its bacon and eggs (which were almost as bad as the coffee), but because of the young brunette with a smile full of the whitest teeth: that contrast was the most beautiful thing the regular had ever seen. She would smile whenever he said something funny, and he learned to say funny things just to see her smile. It was all goofy, prosaic and sincere. And he would return, every day, like an obsessed cinephile returning to see daily sessions of his favorite film.

Unlike her, and her excessively jealous boyfriend, and their families, the regular customer had *papeles*. Better yet: he was a gringo. American, with American parents and Irish grandparents. So what if he was twenty-something years older than her? He had a three-bedroom house in Tallahassee, with a new television and a lovely lawn that he cut regularly with his electric Black & Decker lawnmower.

When the illegal Salvadorian immigrant and the gringo got married, they put a second car in the garage and the two cars had matching colors and personalized number plates HIS XO and HERS XO. It had been her idea. She liked the way gringos used "X" and "O" to indicate kisses and hugs (she wasn't sure of the order). Putting kisses and hugs on the bumper was a way of fraternizing with the world. Socializing her happiness in HIS and HERS license plates.

They bought a second television, so they could each watch their programs without any conflicts. And she didn't even need to work anymore. She could stay at home looking after the kids, when kids came along.

But before kids came the ex-chambermaid and ex-waitress's mother and father, whom she brought out from Colorado and installed in the spare bedroom.

Then all the mutual hurt melted away in the cheery Florida sun, which was so different to the semiarid Colorado sun, so much better, so much more humanitarian. The Colorado sun used a whipping stick and had downward-curving lips, between literal mountains of wrinkles. The Florida sun served orange juice processed with a smile, in sandals and shorts, very informal. And it didn't aspire to be Icelandic in the winter.

The family would find happiness there. But eight years earlier no one had any way of knowing it.

Corvus corax, Corvus brachyrhynchos

WHEN FERNANDO, HER future husband and future ex-husband, went to live in the Amazon, to rehearse and stage the guerrilla war, my mother was nine years old and was moving with her geologist father to another country. The fact that this other country had dangerous ties to the military coup in Brazil and with everything that Fernando, gun in hand, was fighting, was curious, nothing else. How could Suzana have imagined, at the age of nine, a former communist guerrilla as a husband?

Not that she knew these words intimately, not that she knew their meaning. All she knew was what her father told her: that the communists were bad people.

She saw an astronaut from her new country plant her new country's flag in lunar soil, in the month of July. She thought it strange and beautiful. She had heard of Woodstock and the jungles of Vietnam, but they were at the periphery of her interests, and it made no difference to her when Nixon addressed the "silent majority" in a request for support for the war. She didn't consider herself silent, suspected she wasn't part of the majority and didn't know exactly what war was. Besides which she was only nine, and she wasn't entirely sure that Nixon was addressing nine-year-old girls in his speech.

One day she secretly looked at photos of the village of My Lai in *Life* magazine – when the massacre finally came to light, to then disappear from public consciousness, with only the occasional short-lived outbreak of remembering.

The bodies, that pile of mangled bodies. Vietnamese: women, the elderly, children. Babies. Strange words: civilians tortured, raped, beaten, mutilated, because they were suspected of hiding Vietcong among them. (She knew what Vietnamese were, not Vietcong. She asked her father, without mentioning *Life*. Communists from those parts, he said.) Burned houses. Dead, mutilated domestic animals. She wondered if domestic animals could also be communists. Perhaps in Vietnam. Perhaps their owners trained them for it. To recognize non-communists by their smell and attack them. The cows with their hooves and horns. The dogs with their teeth. And so on.

She found out later that Lieutenant William Calley, who had led the My Lai massacre, served only three and a half years house arrest of his original life sentence. The memorial in My Lai, Vietnam, listed more than five hundred dead, with ages ranging from one to eighty. In Suzana and her father's new country, some were indignant that Calley was the only one punished. Even Vietnam War veterans. Others considered him a patriot and a hero, because in a war, after all, you respond to enemy fire as best you can. Even when there is no enemy fire. The answer needn't need to follow the question – and the ends, of course, justify the means.

My mother told me about the color photographs of My Lai in *Life* magazine and about Nixon talking to the astronauts on the moon. It was while we were on holiday in Barra do Jucu. We were on the beach and it was night. She was holding a can of beer and telling me things from when she was a child. I don't remember all of them. I remember that night, the cool breeze and my hot skin; I remember the color of the beer can, I remember the sky and the stars over Barra do Jucu and the photos that I hadn't seen in *Life* magazine and the speech that I hadn't heard Nixon deliver. But at any rate, between the things you remember and those you don't, between the things you know and those you don't, you have to plug the holes with whatever is at hand. And perhaps any attempt to know someone else is always that, your hands trying to shape three-dimensionality, your desire and incompetence putting together a scrapbook to bring to life someone who is dead, a friend, a mysterious lover who goes over to the window at first light and stands there gazing into space, without uttering a word. An unsociable child, a terse teacher, a humorless workmate who stares at you with a deadpan face when you tell an irresistible joke. People you don't know or with whom you don't feel comfortable. Everyone.

According to the photos, my mother's legs and arms went on forever, and so did her hair. Her face was Latino and ordinary.

My face is Latino and ordinary. I look at the photograph in the passport with which I entered the United States of America nine summers ago.

I see my mother in my own eyes. Missing her no longer inhibits my life. Thinking about who she might have been. What she might have looked like. It's no longer a myth.

I saw my mother in my own eyes for the first time when I was flicking through my passport, organizing the things in my backpack as I touched down in Denver. Nine years ago. The woman next to me told me to use lots of moisturizer.

At the airport I passed a girl who was crying. She was wearing an orange dress with a tiny flower print. She had curly blonde hair. Her eyes were red and there were circumstantial wrinkles on her forehead. She was quite young. Then I caught a little train to the other side of the airport and got off when a voice on the PA system said welcome to Denver and some other things that I didn't understand.

My mother was quite young when she met Fernando in a London pub, she on vacation with her American boyfriend, he with pints of beer in his hands instead of weapons. There he was: drifting, an anomalous fish in a tank of distant beings. There he was: an apparition, a miracle, his body alive and whole, which, for obvious reasons, it shouldn't have been. There he was, singing English music in a low voice and off-key because a while ago he had stopped caring if he sang out of tune.

He saw her and decreed the continuation of the world, the extension of time. The incorruptibility of the heart, which has its own methods and its own ethics, like any other muscle, come to think of it. He saw her and thought he needed, desperately, something to think about.

He had needed something to think about for years and had only just realized it. He needed a territory in which to hew trails in order to recognize himself again. It had been years since he'd felt the familiar weight of a weapon. It had been years since he'd felt the need to love a woman except for the purposes of subsistence, merely to avoid the armlock of loneliness.

Things were swamped by a white desert that came from inside him and spread outwards, a contagious, viral desert, where sounds were diffuse, flavors were shallow, sight was limited.

And life was a contradiction of terms: years earlier he had left his life behind in order to stay alive, and this functional, illogical equation gave him daily electric shocks in the open wounds that he didn't have from the suicide that he hadn't tried to commit.

Perhaps it would be like this forever and perhaps merely existing wasn't enough, even with custom-made shoes and thermostat-regulated temperatures. But he saw Suzana and talked to her, and if desire and the desire for happiness were fake, there was only one way to find out.

You're not from here. Your accent is different, she told Fernando.

He looked at the girl with the Latino face and American voice and said, trying to sound as British as possible, that she wasn't from there either and her accent was different too.

She turned around and he said in Portuguese but you're the most beautiful woman in this place.

She wasn't. That's why she didn't hear him. But she came back later for more beers and said your face is really Brazilian.

And she came back the next day, after a fight with her American boyfriend. And later she and Fernando got drunk together with the objective of turning the world into something fluid, and as the sun tried to rise through a drifting London fog they fell asleep fully dressed and drunk in one another's arms and woke up thirsty and with headaches and it was only then that they undressed each other. And it was only then that Suzana felt enormously guilty about the boyfriend, and Fernando accepted the fact that he'd have to follow her to the United States. Like someone receiving a list of duties on the first day of a new job.

On the other end of the line, Elisa cried almost every time. That's why I preferred letters. Every two weeks I remembered to fill two sheets of paper with a handful of consistent information about school, home, the weather, the ultimate team, the mutant trees rusting the sidewalks and the neighbor's back yard, the books, Fernando, Aditi, Carlos at some point, Nick at some point, the dentist at some point, my father's mother at some point.

I was hoping to save some money to come visit you at Christmas but it's a bit hard.

On the other end of the line she'd cry a little.

Tell me you're OK.

I'm fine, Elisa.

Then she'd ask to speak to Fernando and they'd talk for an average of four minutes.

Every two weeks I received a letter from Elisa talking about work, home, the beach, the weather, at some point a man she'd met – the son of an elderly woman I'm caring for, he seems like a decent person and he's asked me out to dinner on Saturday. I don't know if I'll accept his invitation. I think I'll accept it but I'll let him ask again so he won't think I'm too available, you know. Men like it when we play hard-to-get. If you're too easy it's no fun.

Carlos peered at the letter. He pointed at the Portuguese word for "work", *trabalho*, mouthed the Spanish *trabajo*, and grinned. He pointed at the word for "time", *tempo*, and mouthed *tiempo*. He asked me what *filho* meant. *Hijo*, I said, and he was a little disappointed by the lack of obvious similarities.

I asked Carlos if he had grandparents. He nodded and I noticed that the lenses of his glasses were filthy.

Give me those.

I washed his glasses with dishwashing liquid in the kitchen sink and dried them on the tea towel.

He told me he had two sets of grandparents and that when he was big he was going to visit them but that at the moment he couldn't leave America because if he did he wouldn't be able to return. He could only leave the day he had *papeles*. His father had explained it to him. It was important to stay in America and get *papeles*. His father had told him that it would be easier if he studied, so he was studying. Hard.

The image of a crow stared at us from the computer screen. Carlos had to do a school project about some kind of bird, and he'd chosen the crow.

He asked me if I knew that crows were really intelligent. And if I knew that some crows also ate dead animals. And that many species had become extinct after humankind colonized places like New Zealand and Hawaii.

(Where's New Zealand? he asked. I went to get an atlas and opened it in front of him. It's far away. You have to cross the ocean to get there. I covered the name on the map with my finger. What's this ocean called? I tested him. He gave a start and answered Pacific! with a nervous, credulous cry. While he was there he also observed that New Zealand was also far away from Brazil and El Salvador, where his grandparents were awaiting his visit the day he had *papeles*. Then he asked me if I thought there were any boys from New Zealand who didn't have *papeles* in Colorado.)

Carlos told me that there were the *cuervos* that *los gringos* call crows and the *cuervos* that *los gringos* call ravens. Not the same. See: here *los* raven, *Corvus corax*. Here *los* crow, *Corvus brachyrhynchos*.

According to the library book, the raven is a meditative, aloof individual that you find in deserts, in the tundra, on plains and in forests, in large, open, more or less unoccupied spaces. It is a large black bird with a wedge-shaped tail and feather necklace. It mates, though it is not known if it does so for life. There are signs that couples last at least a year. Both parents care for their young, many of which die in their first few years of life. According to research, individuals living in the wild can live for as many as thirteen years. In captivity, as many as eighty (in the Tower of London, where their wings are clipped in the name of tradition, so they can come and go but not too much, the oldest lived until it was forty-four). It does not migrate, but can travel short distances to avoid climatic extremes. It doesn't live in flocks. It prefers solitude or, at the most, lives in pairs. It likes to hover in the sky, as if the air were a large

unmarked plain and it weighed nothing. It eats practically everything: fruit, shoots, cereals, insects, amphibians, birds, reptiles,
carrion. It even eats other animals that eat carrion. It would seem
that the *Corvus corax* is a serious bird that respects life and death.

According to the book, the crow is an equally black bird that
you find in open spaces with trees nearby. It also feels at home in
urban spaces – in suburbs, parks, coastal towns. Its feathers are
lustrous. Iridescent. It is smaller than its raven cousin. It has strong
claws and, when young, blue eyes, that later darken. When it is
born, it is fed by its parents and older siblings. It can live for up to
fourteen years in the wild. In captivity it lives for an average of
twenty years. In the crow's complex social system, adults stay fairly
close to the place of their birth and often don't mate, instead helping to take care of other crows' young. Sometimes they migrate in
flocks. The *Corvus brachyrhynchos* is omnivorous. It eats insects and
their larvae, carrion, mice and frogs and rabbits, eggs stolen from
smaller birds' nests, fruits and nuts and cereals, and anything it can
find in an unwatched trash can.

Carlos's mother was still in hospital but according to him she
would be home on Monday. She would arrive thinner, with dark
little valleys under her eyes and two invisible hands pushing her
shoulders down and forward, aging her, subordinating her. And
she would say she wanted to return to San Salvador, but she would
say it without shouting, because by now she had learned how
dangerous it was to resort to too many decibels and attract the
neighbors' attention, in a place where people really do call the
police and the police really do come. A few days later, she would
invite the persistent pamphlet lady into her house and talk about

god. She would argue that if god really existed she would be back in San Salvador. With her daughter. And the pamphlet lady would talk about the inscrutability of His designs. Later, in Florida, Carlos's mother would recover her faith and forgive god.

Carlos printed out the bird photographs that he found during his research. The big *Corvus corax*, solitary and remote, ravens. The *Corvus brachyrhynchos*, crows, with their cooperative souls and knack for trash cans. Then he hugged me and said he missed his sister and asked me for some *guaraná*.

I gave him a little and told him that with any luck he'd soon be able to go visit his sister in Florida. As soon as things settled down a little.

And he told me that sure, why not, but that afterwards he'd come back. He wanted to live and die in Colorado and if possible close to me.

Then he asked Fernando, who was watching us from the couch, if he thought I was going to die four years before him because I was four years older than him. And Fernando replied that things didn't work like that. And Carlos thought about it for a moment and said, like someone handing down a sentence, that it was true, he was right.

Carlos spent that night with us, after asking his father for permission, and asked if we could stay up until midnight. We watched TV and played cards and before midnight he had already fallen asleep on the couch with his mouth open, snoring softly. We put a pillow under his spiky hair, took off his glasses and covered him with a blanket.

★ ★ ★

The next day, a Sunday, Fernando went out early. I didn't know why. Maybe he had gone for a swim at the public swimming pool – the one that was indoor and heated and thus didn't stay closed to the public for eight months of the year. It was more or less his version of a social life. He would swim a couple of miles amidst other semi-sub-aquatic arms and legs and would come home smelling of chlorine and hang a towel smelling of chlorine in the bathroom.

He left a note on the table. It didn't explain anything. It just said LOOK OUTSIDE. Carlos was still asleep, so I carefully opened the front door of the still-groggy house.

Outside a white film had settled over all things: trees, cars, roofs, the street, sidewalks. Tiny, fuzzy, pallid objects were floating down from the sky, noiselessly and almost weightlessly. Some even rose again in the air, halfway down, as the faintest current of air flicked them up invisibly. Then they drifted down again. Then up again. Like children at a party. I crouched down, scooped up a handful of the whipped cream that had piled up at the front door and squeezed it. The cold hurt. The air cut my face; it entered my nostrils and lungs with tiny knives. Everything allowed itself to be covered by that substance that until then, for me, had only existed in films and books, an anti-tropical substance.

When the red Saab pulled up in front of the house a short time later, Carlos and I were outside, captivated by that climatic phenomenon that, historically, had so little to do with us.

My ears hurt and my cheeks hurt. My face was red and my nose was running. There was a first-time joy inside me, a kind of euphoric calm. I was the boy from the country who gazes at the ocean and wonders how it doesn't overflow. I was the peasant who stares at a skyscraper and wonders how it doesn't fall down. And Carlos looked at me, immensely happy at my happiness, and told me that it had been like that for him the first time too.

I think we're going to have to buy those boots now, said Fernando as he passed. He smelled of chlorine. He grabbed a handful of snow and rubbed it on my head, and I protested without protesting.

That night I dreamed of the cold. It was a harsh cold, the cold of a world that scoffed at the naked bipeds who thought they were the boss of it. It was a whole, chaste cold. Without the convenience of heated homes. A cold without contours, without seasons and counter-seasons; just cold. I wasn't part of the dream. Neither was Fernando, or Carlos, or his family, or my possible father, or my mother, or anyone. The cold didn't need people to dream it up.

That morning a plateau of snow had appeared in front of the house. The snow conspires with the desert. Things lose their contours and the all-white sky sticks to the all-white roof, making worlds coincide, annulling distances. There is something of a unifying dream in it, like Esperanto. There were no longer any colors. Everything was the silent accumulation of the snowflakes that fell, tiny and incessant, as tenaciously as death takes over a body. But we were alive, and inside the house the comfort and warmth felt prodigal. Or insulting.

Fernando put his coffee mug on the table. He pulled on his boots, got a wide shovel and said I'm going outside to clear the white shit off the sidewalk.

I thought he'd apologize for saying shit, but he didn't.

★ ★ ★

A few days in a row of insistent snow (and a snow storm on the Thursday that left everyone stranded in their houses, schools closed, Fernando unable to go to work) had turned bald slopes into runs that children plumped out in colorful jackets slid down on colorful sleds. That was when Fernando came home with the red plastic sled and, promising me that I wasn't going to die, pushed me down the slope.

I opened my mouth on the way down and swallowed enough snow to perform a kind of self-baptism. From then on I was one of them. I was the same. I was just another girl in a light purple waterproof jacket, and black rubber boots lined with synthetic fur. And jeans stiff with cold to which snow bandages stuck. And mittens. And a stocking hat with two braids at the sides. The jacket and boots were from an outlet but they were good quality, although it felt strange to have all those textures between my skin and the world. I now existed in layers.

The air became hard again, but the essence of this hardness was different. At any rate, I needed to accept that there was rarely any middle ground in that place. And at any rate what mattered was that now I was one of them, yes: analogous, comparable to, like. In a prosaic fraternity of jacket-encased bodies sliding down smooth white slopes, amidst awe-inspiring spills and war cries. I too uttered cries, I too took spills, I too.

Carlos closed his eyes and I said open your eyes, Carlos, it's no fun with your eyes closed, and in one of his spills he lost his glasses and we desperately hunted for a long time until we saw an arm sticking out of a mound of soft snow like a periscope.

The pine trees dotted around us reminded me of the plastic

Christmas trees that my mother and I used to decorate with cotton in December. The sky was blue, but the sun was angled. It got into my eyes from underneath, almost, as if its rays were flexible. It bumped into the mountains at five o'clock. Airplanes left white tracks in the sky, and distant trails of sound, which arrived with a delay.

Fernando and I arranged the trip to New Mexico for the end of November, when I had a week off school for Thanksgiving.

I felt like a stage actress on opening night. I was backstage applying makeup, getting dressed, mentally going over my lines, warming up my voice, Peter Piper picked a peck of pickled peppers, a peck of pickled peppers Peter Piper picked, if Peter Piper picked a peck of pickled peppers, then where's the peck of pickled peppers Peter Piper picked, as I had seen my mother's friend's actor friend do once backstage at the Glaucio Gill Theatre in Copacabana. (Moments later I saw him on the stage, transfigured: confident and handsome in the limelight. It had to be possible.)

The dog-eared maps of Colorado and New Mexico were reinforced with sticky tape. They left the drawer and migrated to the glove box of the Saab.

Fernando went to Carlos's house personally to ask his parents for permission to take him with us, at my insistence (he'll be so lonely, Fernando, a whole week with no school, and do you think his folks are going to take him out anywhere?).

Carlos's eyes shone as if someone had switched them on. But his eternal concern led him to ask if he needed *papeles* to go to New Mexico, and if he did, what should he do.

His father's moustache said, in tight-lipped Spanish, that Carlos shouldn't go around saying things like that. People turned other people in (no, he wasn't referring to us – of course not – we were friends – but Carlos had a loose tongue). And if that were to happen, if someone were to turn them in, they would have to leave. LEAVE. And worse, they'd have to leave Dolores behind, because now she was in Florida leading a different life. And they might never see Dolores again if they had to leave for some reason. Carlos's mother started to sniffle and covered her face with her hands. Fernando cleared his throat and stared at the wall. Carlos was immediately gripped with panic, apologized and never uttered the word *papeles* again.

At that moment he grew a little more, confirming my theory that that was how things went, in bursts, in spasms, and not in arithmetic continuity. All of the metaphors for growth – the steps on a ladder, a road with curves here and there – were sheer nonsense. It all really happened in fits and starts, like when I was on the plane going to the United States and at some point they told us to fasten our seatbelts because we were going to hit some turbulence, and suddenly that aerial pachyderm which, according to Americans, had been invented by the Wright brothers started to shake in the middle of the sky. It shook as if there were potholed asphalt beneath it, like on certain stretches of the highway between Rio de Janeiro and Barra do Jucu.

In the blink of an eye, a cloud, a sister who leaves home with her boyfriend, a sentence someone says involving *papeles* and suddenly you are older. Depending on the turbulence, maybe it is possible to go to bed at the age of forty and wake up sixty.

★   ★   ★

My mother should have stayed married to you, I told Fernando the night before we left, as we were eating the pasta that I had prepared myself with a sauce with Paul Newman's face on the label.

How do you know that she was the one who ended it?

Was it you?

I stared at him with a pair of perplexed eyes and he laughed.

No. It was her. Suzana was the one who ended it. After a while it's not important anymore, who ended it, who didn't. At any rate, things with her were like that. Wonderful while they lasted. But they didn't last long.

He cut his pasta with his knife, as my mother had taught me not to do. You roll it up on your fork like this, she used to say. It was quite a bit of work. When I saw Fernando cutting his pasta with his knife I decided to cut mine too. Etiquette was silly.

Your mother had some cycles, I think. Seasons. From time to time she needed to change essential things in her life and sometimes these essential things involved other people.

Was it the same with my father?

I don't know if it was the same with your father. She and I were married on paper, you know. She changed her surname and everything. On our wedding day she wore a white dress and a flower in her hair, and we went to a beer garden to celebrate with her friends. We were married for six years. I think she only spent a few months with Daniel.

In the spaces between Fernando's words, in his gestures, in the way his eyebrows danced above his eyes like lizards doing ballet, I realized that he wanted to lay claim to at least that: the position of most-important-man.

The man Suzana had MARRIED wearing a WHITE DRESS
and a flower in her hair.

Were you jealous?

'Course not. I never even met Daniel. I moved here to Colorado
when your mother and I split up. The next week. I spent a few
days in the hotel, over in Albuquerque, and then I came. I got a job
in Aurora.

Doing what?

One thing or another.

Six years is quite a long time.

That depends. It can be a long time or it can be almost nothing.

Did you still love her?

He didn't look at me. He shrugged and said yes.

Then you must have been jealous.

Maybe. It's possible.

I sighed. I didn't know if we should be having this conversation.
I cut some more pasta and put it in my mouth.

My mother was kind of complicated, I said.

She was, said Fernando.

Las Animas

ON THE MAP the Interstate 25 led honestly south, until it ran into the dotted line where Colorado met New Mexico, eye to eye, foreheads aligned.

We had five or six hours of driving ahead of us. We stopped to fill the tank at the first gas station and Carlos wanted to buy some chocolate with some of the twelve dollars of spending money he had brought with him. Fernando bought three bottles of water and a bag of really bad salsa chips. The packet said: MADE WITH REAL AVOCADOS AND TOMATOES. But they tasted like anything but real avocados and tomatoes. I bought a pair of slightly embarrassing sunglasses with pink and blue frames. Then I waited for the sun to come out so I could wear them. But the morning was taking its time, as if dragging itself out of an autumn night with wintry aspirations was slow and a little painful.

Carlos had telephoned the previous evening to list off the items in his suitcase and ask if I agreed. His mother had helped him choose them, but he wanted to be extra-super-sure that his suitcase contained everything necessary. He didn't want to have to reuse underwear or socks on such an important trip.

Such an important trip: for the surprise-reasons nestled in the days to come, waiting for their moment to leap out. Panting trapeze artists with drums beating down below.

Carlos didn't know anything. We hadn't told him anything about anything. But the trip was important according to his own personal parameters. It was an event. It was the first time in his life, for example, that he had been away from his itinerant family.

It was a little after seven o'clock. Fernando had hauled me out of bed at six-thirty and pushed me out of the house at seven. It was still dark when I got up. In the merciless cold that preceded the dawn, the world was full of placid suspense; supernatural minus the ghosts. It turned its face unhurriedly toward the sun that would appear when it had to, no sooner, no later.

We stopped the Saab in front of Carlos's house, before a mosaic of sparse plant-life and small puddles of hard snow. Carlos walked down to the street holding hands with his dad. His face was solemn: he was perhaps a brave little soldier setting out to save the nation. A pre-hero in a stocking hat and gloves. He smelled vaguely of aftershave. As we greeted one another, pale steam came out of our mouths. The sky was a two-dimensional, milky, dull surface.

The two adults made pale, steamy comments about the weather. There was no snow predicted for that week and it was going to be a good week, and the roads would be good. The red Saab rumbled quietly, its motor running, a testament to its serenity and discipline.

Carlos's dad told us to have a good time and to call to check in. The two adults shook hands, Carlos jumped into the car and the moon remained steadfast in the colorless sky, entirely oblivious to whatever was going on beneath it.

After a little while, Carlos asked to see the map and was elated when he realized that before getting to Santa Fé we would pass through Las Vegas.

Fernando had to explain that it wasn't the Las Vegas he was thinking of, which was in Nevada not New Mexico, and Carlos lowered his eyes to the map again, vaguely disappointed.

Then, mentally inaugurating an improbable chapter of tourism in our lives, he suggested that we go to the real Las Vegas the next time there was a long weekend. Or to New York, another city he'd heard a lot about.

Half an hour later, he was asleep in the back seat of the Saab, lying down with his knees pulled up to his tummy, glasses crooked on his forehead.

The Saab broke down near Starkville, in the country of Las Animas. We were about twenty minutes from the state border. Fernando swore in Portuguese and Carlos may have understood him. We had traveled two hundred miles in three and a half hours, taking into account the pee-stop we had made outside Pueblo.

At the beginning of the trip, Carlos slept for over an hour, while I tracked the Saab's freefall down the map. We left Castle Rock and Larkspur behind us. In front of the Air Force Academy at the entrance to Colorado Springs, I noticed that the highway took on the name Ronald Reagan Highway. Pikes Peak loomed above us, a proudly tall mountain in a land of tall mountains. We left the city and its Saturday morning behind.

Haven't you ever wanted to go back to Brazil? I asked Fernando.

I've thought about it a few times.

So why haven't you ever gone back?

There isn't much for me in Brazil.

What do you mean, there isn't much for you in Brazil? You're from there. You left because you had to.

Truth be told, Vanja, I wasn't forced to leave. I left because I wanted to. I know I once told you that, that I had to leave. But no one sent me away, and other people in the same situation stayed. They're still around. Some are in the government. They paid a price, of course. But I did too.

Fine, but if you didn't leave you might have had problems. With the police. The army, I mean. You said so yourself.

He sighed.

If I were in Brazil today I might very well be working as a security guard and cleaner too. Who knows. But life would be a little more difficult.

You could do something else. Maybe you'd be in the government too. Imagine! You might be a federal deputy, a minister.

He laughed.

I don't know if I'd want to do anything else. Or if I'd be able to. Maybe serve beers in a bar.

That's not the only thing you've done in your life. You studied geography.

I did a year of geography.

But you've done other things.

Sure. I attended the Peking Military Academy. And I was a communist guerrilla. That's the most important part of my CV.

I didn't say anything.

After a time he added: I don't need to tell you that these things have to stay between us, right?

He didn't. We overtook a car carrier transporting a cluster of cars with dents in different places and to different degrees. One of them was missing its front bumper, which made it look like a mutilated face, the sort you see close-up in horror movies, a bulging headlight like an eye in a bed of live flesh. I liked talking to Fernando.

A black car overtook us. There was a National Rifle Association sticker on the back window, with an eagle perched on two crossed rifles against a red background.

There is something intermediary about deserts. Many travelers have said it. It is as if they weren't destinations, just routes. Great inhospitable landscapes where you don't dawdle, you just travel from one more affable point on the map to another. And yet people live there. People live in the world's deserts and arid and semiarid wildernesses. In these places between parentheses. Where all things – sounds, distances – inhabit other semantics. It seems like a desperate gesture. Or perhaps an abandonment.

I hate this place, Nick once told me.

What place? School?

Colorado.

You hate it? Why?

You walk and there's nothing. You drive for hours and hours and there's nothing. Just some bushes on the ground. I wish I lived somewhere where there were trees.

There are the mountains, I mused.

The mountains, he said. A bunch of pine trees and ski stations. Rich folk's mansions imitating Swiss chalets. No thanks.

I made a mental note that Nick wasn't interested in pine trees, ski stations or rich folk's mansions imitating Swiss chalets.

This all used to be underwater, I said, happy with the knowledge I had recently acquired from the Science Museum. You know, thousands of years ago. It was all ocean.

As far as I'm concerned it might as well still be, he said.

In the car with Fernando, I thought about the Colorado sea, and what animals might have lived there, in that deserted terrain that the highway cut through in an infinite straight line as if to say, OK, if you want to keep going, it's your problem – let's see what you're capable of. What shells of Mesozoic dimensions, what strange animals living inside them.

What are you to me? I asked Fernando.

What?

What are you to me? Because according to my birth certificate you're my dad, but you're not my real dad, so what are you?

He looked at me, then back at the highway, the persistent gray strip of highway and the tufts of scorched vegetation that flanked it, and the blobs of snow here and there, where the sun allowed it.

I don't know. Whatever you want me to be, he replied.

The man at the motel reception desk had gray hair tied back in a pony tail and nicotine-stained teeth. He said there was a heated indoor swimming pool that was open until 9 p.m.

On the side of the counter was a collection of pamphlets about the attractions of Las Animas County. Carlos took one of each and tugged on my arm to show me what they said about the ghost towns. He read out their names: Berwind, Delagua, Ludlow, Morley, Primero, Segundo, Tabasco, Tercio.

And he appeared to like the sound of those words, in that exact order, because he repeated them a few more times. Berwind, Delagua, Ludlow, Morley, Primero, Segundo, Tabasco, Tercio. Berwind, Delagua, Ludlow, Morley, Primero, Segundo, Tabasco, Tercio.

The motel pool was a giant slab of warm water next to the reception, behind a dirty glass wall. There was a young woman with two little boys there when we arrived. The boys stared at us. They were wearing inflatable orange armbands and had skinny legs sticking out of their shorts, and thin chests out of which jutted skinny arms and thin necks and startled oval heads.

A sign said NO LIFEGUARD ON DUTY.

Carlos jumped into the water, a stocky little torpedo with a crew cut. The boys kept staring, unabashed.

Fernando sat on the edge of the pool and didn't take off his shirt. He didn't take off his shirt until the young woman and the little boys had gone, dragging dirty white towels behind them – miniature ghosts exiled from the ghost town, souls in Las Animas, trying to recover their lost privacy. Then Fernando got into the pool and taught Carlos how to do underwater somersaults, which Carlos ended up mastering after inhaling a decent amount of warm, chlorinated liquid through his nostrils and emerging hurt and confused.

In the bedroom, we had two beds. One for Fernando, one for me and Carlos.

Fernando ordered pizza, beers and sodas. The three of us

distractedly watched a film for adolescents on TV as we ate, Carlos and I lying belly-down on our bed and getting ketchup and mustard on the bedspread, Fernando at a round table with one leg shorter than the others that rocked back and forth every time he leaned on it.

Carlos put on his space-themed pajamas. It had astronauts and stars against a black background, and six-legged extraterrestrials with tufts of antennae on their heads and goofy smiles. He brushed his teeth with his new toothbrush, which he had bought specially for the trip.

Later, in the dark, I heard his heavy, just-fallen-asleep breathing.

On the other bed, Fernando was an indistinct shape, motionless, as if he had ceased to exist. As if he had left his body there and gone off to do something else.

On the highway outside night trucks and cars carrying tired eyes behind steering wheels drove past. Each of them was a broad noise and a flash of light. Low-pitched noises and king-size flashes of light for the trucks. Higher-pitched noises and more discreet flashes of light for the cars.

I fell asleep and dreamed of a pool, at the bottom of which were tunnels leading to other pools. The water carried Carlos's liquid voice repeating the names of the ghost towns of Las Animas County.

I leapt out of the dream and fully woke up a short time later, when I heard someone knocking on the door of the room next to ours. Fernando was still in the same position, the same inexistence. I realized he was awake, because sleeping bodies tend to be easier, more abandoned objects – like Carlos beside me. I rolled over in bed and leaned on my elbow.

Fernando?

Hmm?

Aren't you sleepy?

No.

Want some gum?

No. Thanks.

Nick didn't like people who chewed gum and he could never find out about the little strawberry-flavored packet that lived in the bottom of my bag.

Did you tell my mother what happened to you when you left Brazil?

Fernando was fully dressed, lying on top of the bedspread, the bed still made. His shoes, on the ground, looked like giant sleeping beetles, with the appendages of their laces hanging at their sides.

Some of it, he said. Not everything.

Do you think much about it?

I used to. Not so much anymore.

Don't you like to think about it?

At this stage, it doesn't make much difference. You know? Thinking about it or not thinking about it.

We stayed there like that, awake and silent for a while, listening to Carlos breathe. Listening to the noises from the highway. A digital clock with scarlet letters on the bedside table showed 23:11.

Could you pass me a beer? Fernando asked.

I got a beer from the dwarf fridge that was snoring with its dwarf asthma next to my bed. Fernando opened the can with a metallic sneeze and took a sip.

Do you want me to tell you the things I never told your mother?

I was quiet and listened. For a good while, I just listened.

I never asked Fernando why he decided to talk that night. If, by any chance, he had decided to indemnify my mother for the things he hadn't told her by telling her daughter. But if I asked he probably would have said: at this stage, it doesn't make much difference.

I was awoken shortly after 8am by Carlos tugging on my big toe. I felt like hitting him. But I just grumbled and pulled my foot up and rolled over to keep sleeping.

He and Fernando were already up, dressed and groomed. Fernando was wearing the birthday T-shirt. The coffee-maker was making coffee as it always did, as it was condemned to do for countless guests, day after day, gurgling and blowing out steam on the counter between the toothbrushes. The coffee came in sachets, the sugar and sweetener in little packets.

I knew it must be time to get up. We ate a trio of bagels in the motel foyer on Styrofoam plates and used plastic knives to spread on the cream cheese and jam that came in tiny individual plastic packages. We drank a little processed juice from Styrofoam cups and more coffee in other Styrofoam cups. By the time we had finished we had three Styrofoam plates, six Styrofoam cups, three plastic knives, three plastic spoons, a few empty packets of sugar and some empty cream cheese and jam packages to throw in the trash. After that, we had a car to get from the workshop and a trip to resume.

Las Animas bordered on New Mexico. At the top of Raton Pass, Carlos wanted to stop, get out of the car and take photographs at the state border. Then he asked Fernando what New Mexico had to do with Mexico.

Camino Sin Nombre

WE MET JUNE in Santa Fé a day late. Fernando had let her know that the car had broken down. Late that Sunday morning, there were tourists in the main square buying silver and turquoise jewelry made and sold by the Indians. Women in fur coats and leather boots strolled about in pairs, followed by men in cowboy hats, who paid for the things their wives bought and carried the bags.

The Indians spread out their earrings and necklaces and bracelets on colorful blankets, on designated sidewalks, next to the wall of the Palace of the Governors. They also wrapped themselves in colorful blankets if it was cold, and some ate the food they had brought from home.

In the surrounding area, the stores inhabited adobe constructions. They sold Native American art and Rolex watches.

June's father, she told us later, was a descendent of the Zuni nation. June's mother was an English linguist who had gone to New Mexico to study the Zuni language, Shiwi'ma, an isolated indigenous language according to scholars. She didn't find any answers, but she found a man she liked (who wasn't fluent in Shiwi'ma, because he had grown up outside of the pueblos, but who had his own particular, paralinguistic attractions).

June's mother returned to England with June's father by her side and June in her belly.

But after New Mexico, England seemed excessively wet, excessively tame. Subtle. European. June learned to play the piano, June's father got a job, and June's mother continued to study isolated languages.

One fine day, as if it had been agreed upon from the outset, they sold or gave away everything they had, crossed the Atlantic and returned to New Mexico. They passed through the portal that returned them to that climatic and visual violence as one might recover their name or soul. June started teaching piano, put on a little weight and then a little more, and years later inherited her parents' home in Santa Fé. She didn't speak the Zuni language, but she had studied Latin at school, in Oxford.

We arranged to meet at a gas station. Carlos read aloud EXCLUSIVE PARKING FOR TEXACO AND 7-ELEVEN CUSTOMERS. He grew worried because we were taking up a parking spot and we weren't Texaco or 7-Eleven customers. Fernando told him not to worry. But he kept glancing around suspiciously. Perhaps he imagined a police officer was going to come and warn us about our offence and ask to see our *papeles*, as he drummed on the car with his club – like in the movies. Carlos would break into a cold sweat, then he'd cry and then he'd be deported. Like in the movies.

June pulled up next to us. We watched as that enormous, dark-skinned woman got out of her green pickup and leaned over to rest her forearms in Fernando's open window. But she looked at me before she looked at him, and said, in a British accent: Suzana's daughter. Only then did she look at Fernando and say: Suzana's ex-husband. And then, at the back seat: and their little friend. We'd best go indoors somewhere to chat a little. It's cold today. Though you folks from Colorado aren't afraid of the cold. And she smiled, and her smile came with twin dimples, one in each cheek. Aren't you lot hungry? Do you want to have lunch? There's this place I know, it's my treat.

She didn't seem to remember that none of us were, in essence, from Colorado. Our address was there, but that was all. June was wearing a flannel shirt with tiny blue flowers on it and a long, thick skirt. She told us we could follow her. She went back to her green pickup, and as we watched, her backside swayed under her skirt, back and forth, confident and magnificent.

Carlos asked how she knew that we were who we were, quite impressed. And he loved June immediately, for everything: because she smiled, because she had dimples, because she knew that we were who we were. But above all for having said that he was from Colorado. That was what Carlos felt in the pit of his stomach, in his bones, under his nails, in everything that in him served as roots. In Colorado, some people had bumper stickers that said NATIVE. Once Carlos had sworn to me that when he grew up and got his *papeles* and had a car he was going to buy one of those bumper stickers. Because that was how he felt: NATIVE, with mountains in the background. And June had known it just by looking at him, which was enough to make him love her at that very instant.

It still hadn't snowed in Santa Fé and everything was a uniform, thirsty brown. The trees were scrawny. June took us to a restaurant far from the tourist center and said everything's crowded because of the holiday. What do you want? A soda? I'm going to order something a little stronger, and she and her dimples laughed, and when the very young, thin waiter with several piercings in his ear came to take our order she named the wine she was going to have in her semi-British accent. Then she told us, by way of an explanation that we hadn't asked for, that she needed a glass of wine to celebrate, and didn't Fernando want one too? Maybe they could get a bottle? And after the waiter had taken the order she sighed. How lovely to see you. How lovely to see you. And she held my two hands with her two hands on top of the table. Her big, fat, soft hands. My small, thin, rough hands.

We ate nachos that came in a compact mountain and I noticed that Fernando picked out the jalapeños with uncommon avidness. Carlos ordered a milkshake that he couldn't finish. The wine softened June, made her less anxious and talkative, as if it had reduced her rotation speed on a dial. But none of her three table companions was particularly talkative, so it was good to be able to count on her to prevent any likely silences.

After her first glass of wine, we talked about my mother. After the second, we talked about my father. Carlos's eyes bulged. He didn't know that Fernando was my father on my birth certificate (I had been introduced in the neighborhood as a niece). Nor did he know that I had a missing father somewhere on the planet, and that this trip was, in essence, a search.

June explained the unusual situation with the patience of a fourth-grade teacher to the boy who was used to unusual situations.

He nodded his head when he understood, when the revelations stopped elbowing one another in his head and harmonized in their places, fitting together with soft clicks. He held my arm and said he hoped we found my father. I hope we find *tu papá*. How say *papá en portugués*?

June and Fernando polished off the bottle of wine and it became clear to us all that they might order a second and then a third. They didn't. I looked at the thin waiter with piercings in his ear before we left and thought about Nick, whose name was still scribbled on my jeans, next to the drawing of Shah Jahan's diamond.

June wandered the streets of downtown Santa Fé with us, reciting facts and dates with the proficiency of a newly graduated tour guide, zealous and eager to do her job. Living it to the fullest. We went to her house when it started getting dark and too cold. The air was treacherous. It hurt inside my nose. It burned my face. It anesthetized my lips and made us all talk as if we were slightly drunk or just back from the dentist.

She lived on a street named Camino Sin Nombre. Her house had lots of colors inside it and was also inhabited by a pair of mastiffs – Georgia and Alfred. (The O'Keeffe and Stieglitz were inferred by many, but not us, and so June explained about the woman who liked to paint flowers and animal skeletons, and the man who fell in love with the woman who liked to paint flowers and animal skeletons and who photographed her with her hair down in a white shirt. Carlos looked at some reproductions in a book and said that the Georgia lady was a good painter but that he thought those mountains were a bit weird in that painting, they didn't look like real mountains, they looked like little Play-Doh mounds, and why did she paint such big flowers, he personally didn't think flowers were all that interesting.)

June made a dinner that filled the house with warm smells. She put on music and hung invisible hooks in the air that brought us together, threads looped over a crochet needle. We were a world of compatibilities, we were joined, we were equivalent to one another – and where we weren't, we compensated for one another.

One of June's talents: the four of us were suddenly a large, improbable, multinational family, full of different languages and different accents in the same languages. Our ages were rather incompatible in theory, our preoccupations and occupations like-wise, our pasts perhaps identified us as animals of different species, the result of distinct evolutionary processes, and yet there we were. All easy laughter. When no one was looking, I took a swig of wine from Fernando's glass and thought it tasted like grapes with wood and alcohol. It was yucky. And I wondered if you had to swallow liters of grapes with wood and alcohol in order to train your palate or if it changed with age. If one fine day you just woke up liking sex, politics and alcoholic beverages.

The heating in June's house was in the floor – Carlos and I quickly discovered it, the pleasure of walking barefoot on that large, warm, earthy plate. And we quickly realized that, like the painter Georgia, June also liked animal skeletons. There were two skulls in her living room and a small one in the bathroom. The two in the living room had wrinkled horns. The one in the bathroom didn't. While Carlos and I performed a spoof of a ballet on the warm floor, the two old mastiffs watched, perhaps with the vague memory of having done that too at some stage, accompanying other children, in a time when the world had less joint pain.

June went outside for a smoke and Fernando went with her, both holding their drinks. As they were leaving I heard her say: the day before yesterday I saw two coyotes over there.

Later, when I woke up to go to the bathroom, June and Fernando were still talking in the living room, and laughing a lot, and there was a different smell in the air – a sweet smell, which wasn't from a cigarette or incense. I had occasionally smelled it before in Barra do Jucu, during the holidays, at my mother's friends' house. Always after the children were all in bed.

I stopped and listened to Fernando's laughter, that extemporaneous laughter softened by the marijuana, velvety, honest. I remembered my mother's laughter, which was high-pitched and always easy. I closed the bathroom door, sat on the toilet, rested my elbow on the low window and cried a little, and outside there were perhaps two coyotes, treading light and agile in a world all their own.

Tropical forests, like the great recessive Amazon, are intense organisms. Life and death multiply there all the time, simultaneous, Siamese. One spoonfeeds the other. They do it at a routine, everyday pace, without a fuss. A habit that has almost nothing to do with the avatar of death that Fernando had learned to recognize and fear in the forest, when he went by the name of Chico.

In the forest I will be the tree, I will be the leaves, I will be the silence.

In mid-1972, the Armed Forces decided to set up their Civic-Social Actions. They planned vaccination campaigns against syphilis and yellow fever, distributed food by helicopter. The Ministry of Education decided to send money to local schools. The locals were able, thanks to the Civic-Social Actions, to do extravagant things, like get ID cards. Also in this time military repression in the Araguaia region was handed over entirely to the Planalto Military Command.

With the capture of some of the guerrillas, the Army learned things. It discovered, for example, that at night the communists listened to Tirana Radio, from Albania, and Peking Radio, from China. Both broadcast programs in Portuguese with recent news about the Araguaia Guerrilla Movement and left the military perplexed: how on earth did the information get to them? Back at home, the censured press only said what was convenient. But Brazilian Communist Party activists in the cities graffitied walls exalting the guerrilla war and letting everyone know that it was alive and well.

In September, Brazil commemorated the 150th anniversary of its independence from Portugal. With green and yellow flags, there were street celebrations and military orchestras.

In September, a guerrilla from Detachment C wrote a letter to his parents. *May the fascist generals froth with hatred. The revolution is a reality and the people will win. My dear parents, I can't wait for the day to arrive when I can walk into our house, embrace you at long last and say: Here is the triumphant revolution.*

In September, the *Estado de São Paulo*, which received a list of forbidden topics on a daily basis, got around the censorship in an entirely unexpected way. The guerrilla war wasn't on the list one day, so the newspaper published a story entitled "In Xambioá, the struggle is against guerrillas and underdevelopment": *While the joint forces of the Army, Navy and Air Force have approximately five thousand men hunting guerrillas in the jungles of the left bank of the Araguaia River, the Army initiated yesterday, simultaneously, in Xambioá and Araguatins, in the state of Goiás, on the right side of the river in the far north of the state, a Civic-Social Action designed to take assistance to the entire population of the area.* Two days later, the story made the *New York Times.*

The Brazilian Armed Forces had five thousand men hunting a few dozen guerrillas in the forest. By now they also knew that the communists were practicing jungle survival techniques, learning to get their bearings from the sun, stars, and landmarks. Learning to commando crawl in the forest, to recognize edible fruits, to hunt. They knew they were practising target shooting, learning to ambush and storm, studying the enemy. The enemy was studying the enemy, a semantic knot that no one noticed.

Chico wasn't up on these numbers, nor did he know that the guerrillas who had been caught were all sent to the Criminal Investigations Platoon in Brasilia. It was a place where physical and psychological torture methods had been finely tuned. The torturers had PhDs in dragging confessions (which, after all, one doesn't get with bonbons) out of people. Naked and hooded men and women were trussed up and tied to poles where they were variously tortured, held underwater until they almost drowned, and even given electric shocks on their genitals.

According to the Geneva Convention, guerrillas are goners, a
military officer once said to a prisoner in Xambioá.

Now totally stripped of any aspiration to Xangri-Lá, Xambioá,
that hamlet with a population of no more than three thousand, was
often where it began.

One guerrilla from Detachment C, for example, even before she
was sent to Brasilia, discovered hell there on the banks of the
Araguaia, the River of the Macaws. Where the forest should have
been her second mother, where the population was supposed to
support the guerrillas rather than betray them. Stripped naked, she
was punched and kicked in a circle of thirty men. When she was
about to black out, she was taken to the river, where they held her
head under until she almost drowned. Still wet, she was tortured
with electric shocks. Communist whore. They took her to the
river again. And so on. In the intervals, they threw her into a hole,
where the pain and bleeding stopped her from sleeping. According
to the Geneva Convention, guerrillas were goners.

In Xambioá, the army controlled everything and the mayor was
thankful. I've never had it as easy as I do now, he said. How marvel-
ous that the terrorists had chosen to go there, because it was the
only way for a piece of progress to get there too. Highways, medicine. Problems between farmers and squatters resolved in record
time. I need a twenty-mile highway ready within two months said
General Antonio Bandeira, commander of the 3rd Infantry
Brigade, to the chief engineer of the Goiás Highway Department.
The engineer replied that it wouldn't be possible: there wasn't
enough equipment and two months wasn't enough time. You
don't understand, said the general. The highway must be ready in

two months because I'm going to travel along it with my troops. How you do it is your problem.

In September, the rainy season was about to start. Again. Cyclical and indifferent. On the right side of the Araguaia River, in the then state of Goiás, the Civil-Social Action vaccinated more than five thousand locals against yellow fever, and almost three thousand against smallpox. They pulled four thousand teeth. They gave talks on citizenship, hygiene, eating habits, held celebrations, ceremonies, gymkhanas, sporting competitions and even created a youth club after coming to the conclusion that there wasn't much to do in those parts. They donated flags, painted schools, built septic tanks. On the other side of the river, in the state of Pará, dentists attended two hundred locals and doctors saw one thousand, six hundred.

The program lasted eight days. Just as it had all begun, it ended. Eight was also the number of guerrillas killed in the month of September, during Operation Parrot. Among them, João Carlos Haas Sobrinho, a.k.a. Juca, a member of the Military Commission. Before the eight guerrilla deaths in September there had been five others, according to the army, and they had captured more than ten.

Although General Bandeira didn't want it to, the operation ended in early October, by the deadline. The only reason it hadn't been more successful, in his opinion, was because there were too few soldiers for too much forest. The combat area stretched across 3,475 square miles of forest – which they even bombed with napalm in three places. The troops were withdrawing from the Araguaia, leaving behind platoons in three different places with orders to *obtain as much information as possible in order to get a picture of the situation.*

The communists saw the army's retreat as flight. It was a maneuver to avoid demoralization. A mimeographed announcement declared the Guerrilla Forces' intention to go on fighting, and their confidence that they would win. *Death to those who persecute and attack the residents and fighters of the Araguaia!*

In December, the commander of the guerrillas, Maurício Grabois, would send a letter to the party leaders in São Paulo. *We were not isolated (unlike Che in Bolivia), nor did the enemy manage to give the peasants and other inhabitants of the region a false image about us*, he would write, among other positive assessments.

And he would sign off: *Big hugs. A Happy New Year to everyone. 1973 will be a year of victories.*

Any special reason why your mother named you Evangelina?

June was washing up after breakfast and I was helping her.

You know, she continued. Evangelina, evangelism.

I shrugged.

Not that she told me. I think it was just because she liked it. And because it isn't very common. She didn't want me to have a really common name. The same as a whole bunch of other people at school, you know?

As I said this, I remembered the poem a former classmate in Brazil had made up: *A Vanja e o suco de laranja. A Vanja derrama a canja no suco de laranja. A Vanja gosta de canja com suco de laranja.* (Vanja and the orange juice. Vanja spills chicken soup in her orange juice. Vanja likes chicken soup with orange juice.)

Do you have any kids?

I have one, said June. He lives in Kansas.

What does he do there?

He's a musician. He plays the bassoon in the Topeka Symphony Orchestra.

I glanced sideways at June. Maybe she would allow me more questions and even more personal ones. She was the one who had broached the subject.

He was still very little when his father and I got divorced. He was in kindergarten and was an absent-minded kid who was always falling over. He'd fall off the swing at school, he'd fall off his bike, he'd fall down the stairs. Once he broke his two front teeth. Could you put this in the cupboard there please? On the bottom shelf.

And you never married again? I asked.

She cleared her throat. A moment of silence.

I lived with someone for a while. For a good while. Almost fifteen years. But then it ended. As everything does.

Did he leave?

She.

I closed the cupboard door after putting away the jar of ground coffee. I looked at June and said ah, I understand.

The girls at school thought it was gross. A woman with another woman. Not much was said about a man with another man – that was a different kettle of fish, what they did was their problem. But what if your best friend suddenly tried to kiss you and touch your breasts? Or if you suddenly felt inclined to kiss your best friend? Gross gross gross gross gross they would say over and over, as if it were a mantra that could protect them from such great evil. One day I talked to Nick about it. He asked me if I felt like kissing my best friend. No, I said, shrugging, and he said what a shame, that would be really sexy.

What about you? Do you like anyone?

There's a guy at school, I said.

June pointed at the name written on my jeans. Nick?

He's an eco-anarchist.

Really now?

Yep.

And how does an eco-anarchist see things?

I'm not really sure. He lent me a book but I haven't opened it yet.

On the couch, Fernando looked like he was reading the newspaper. Maybe he was. Carlos came back from the bathroom smelling of aftershave. Among his toiletries, which he kept in a clear plastic bag, was a bottle that said *L'Oreal Men's Expert Comfort Max Anti-Irritation After Shave Balm with SPF 15 Sunscreen.*

Let's take the dogs for a walk, said June.

I took Alfred by the collar, Carlos took Georgia and Fernando stayed on the couch, reading the newspaper. The two dogs were old and always sleepy. We walked down Camino Sin Nombre to Martinez Lane, Acequia Madre and Camino Don Miguel, looping back to June's house. Alfred is going to die soon, she said, and I looked at Alfred and thought he knew it too. But time would prove them both wrong. Georgia died first, a few months after our visit. Alfred lived for another two years.

Redondo Road

THE HIGHWAY WAS attached to another highway and then another. It was strange to think about it. Strange and comforting. Of course: there would always be the discontinuity of a dead-end road, here and there. Of a road or street that didn't lead anywhere, that died in a quay or a pasture or a wall of rock. This too was foreseen on maps. One day in the future I would see a tunnel through a mountain in Colorado, near Clear Creek Canyon Road: a tunnel abandoned when the highway was rerouted, black, a mouth excavated in the rock with a wooden fence blocking the bottom. An ex-route.

My father's mother lived on Redondo Road, in Jemez Springs. Our destination, some sixty-five miles from Santa Fé. That was why our highway, on that occasion, needed to be attached to others.

Carlos went with June in her green pickup, allowing him plenty of time with his love at first sight. He wanted to talk to her, hear her talking in that funny English of hers, in her elegant Queen's English, which made him think of jewelry and capes and red velvet. We passed enormous casinos run by the Indians and drove up into the mountains where pine trees grew thankfully, one hundred percent bound to their mountain reality. Much of New Mexico was desert. But not there. We reached Los Alamos and June pulled over to the side of the road. She got out of the car and came to our window.

Los Alamos, she said, you know. And she looked at Fernando and then at me. Did you tell her? We're going to pass through a security gate. They might pull us over, they might not.

No one asked us to stop at the security gate – in fact, there wasn't anyone in any of the cabins – and Fernando provided me with the historical connections that I didn't have, Los Alamos, the Manhattan Project, the atomic bomb, and when he crossed a road called Oppenheimer Drive he explained who Oppenheimer was and said that he had quoted Hindu scripture after the first explosion in New Mexico: *Now I am become Death, the destroyer of worlds.*

It had snowed in Los Alamos. Amid the pine trees there were pale trails of semi-melted snow. I was wearing my sunglasses with the pink and blue frames, and was thinking of the name Oppenheimer. Heimeroppen. Meroppenhei. Enheioppmer.

Now, this woman, this Florence lady, my father's mother, is she expecting us?

No, replied Fernando. But I imagine that people show up at her house from time to time. It's a studio. I don't know what these things are like. I don't know any artists.

I imagine her studio as a large room with a really big dirty table and pieces of newspaper everywhere. Maybe she's hung her favorite poem on the wall. To feel inspired.

Fernando didn't say anything. He didn't say what he imagined Florence's studio would be like. He didn't say if he imagined anything at all. I went along mentally putting together model grandmothers, like in those children's books in which you choose the head on one page and the body on another and the feet on another, and you end up with a cowboy with a ballerina's body and a Martian's feet.

Florence lived on a dirt road. June and Carlos went ahead in the green pickup, blurred by the cloud of dust that they left behind them and which Fernando and I breathed in.

On one side of the road were rocks and vegetation, climbing a steep slope. On the other side was a low concrete wall, between the road and the drop. Every now and then, a house. After we passed the corner of La Cueva Place (a dead-end road, according to the map), June parked the pickup in front of a stone wall – which didn't hide, protect or divide the slope, but merely braced it with the tense tranquility of stones.

An entrance, a low gate. My heart was beating wildly and my hands were cold. We rang the bell and a woman in a wool coat came walking through the garden. She didn't have braids in her hair, nor was it long. It was very short and gray-blonde. There were two small bags under her eyes, and a slightly bigger one under her chin, like a set of ornaments. She wasn't wearing earrings in her ears, rings on her fingers or a watch on her wrist. Her wool coat had a pulled thread near the collar. There were ceramic sculptures standing among the dry plants in her garden. The first my eyes alighted on was a chicken with human genitals. My Woman Chicken, Florence would say later.

Hellooooo, she said in a smile. And who are you?

Ah, said June, waving her hand in a vague gesture that might include Florence's house, us, the whole state of New Mexico, half the planet. We've come to see your studio. We've heard good things about your work and decided to visit. I live in Santa Fé and these are my friends from Colorado.

Florence opened the gate, held out her hand and said Florence.

I looked at her and thought about the children that she might have had. I thought of Florence as a young woman, without the matching bags. I thought of Florence with a swelling belly, her skin stretched and belly-button poking out like an olive, a child completing its pre-natal phases inside.

We crossed the garden of rocks and dry plants and things made of clay. It was as if there was a kind of mistrusting life there. In that garden. Sap hidden behind twiggy stalks, peeking out.

We entered her house and Florence introduced us to her husband. Norbert. (I thought he was my father's father. Later I found out that he was Florence's second husband. They had met eight years earlier, when she was visiting Vermont. Eight years earlier, Florence was a widow and had a sister who lived in Vermont. Norbert was Florence's sister's neighbor, and was also widowed. And Florence could never live in New England. No wet winters for her. No cloudy days.)

Norbert collected vacuum cleaners. Florence introduced us to him in a loud voice because he was a bit deaf. Norbert seemed fifty percent present. His other fifty percent was somewhere else, somewhere that had nothing to do with us. He moved to and fro, from one of his halves to the other, according to simple personal convenience. He had seven different models of vacuum cleaner, which he kept in a special cupboard in the garage. When we entered the house, he was just finishing vacuuming the couch. More than in a clean house, perhaps, he believed in the cleaning potential present in each vacuum cleaner. He believed in what they were capable of doing. In their good souls, so to speak.

As for Florence, she supplemented Norbert's fifty percent presence with another fifty percent. She, too, had another half that was elsewhere, doing ballet somewhere in the space over our heads, and she accompanied the dance of her other detached, traveling self with eyes that never stopped moving. But they weren't nervous eyes, flitting back and forth with no talent for concentration: they were just eyes that undulated, calmly, following some no doubt very beautiful thing that no one else could see. It was the kind of thing that could really bug some people.

I thought that maybe she studied Russian, just for the sake of it, and talked to plants. I thought that maybe she forgot to eat the occasional meal, and at such times Norbert would wander about the house, feeling unhappy and not really sure why he was so hungry.

In her house there was a TV that didn't work and a telephone that she didn't answer. From time to time she would listen to the messages on the answering machine, but she didn't necessarily associate them with any obligation to return calls. There was a gramophone, on which she played operas.

When June had called her a few weeks earlier, it had been like that. A message. A number for Florence to please call back. Florence had listened to the message, registered a group of numbers without any internal logic, and seconds later they had probably broken up like drops of water splattering on the ground, returned to their molecular state, without any other commitment or consequence.

I called a few weeks ago, June said, as Florence was offering us tea (I like to receive everyone that comes to visit my studio with a cup of tea; it's so nice when people come all the way out here – a smile).

Florence clasped her hand. June's soft, chubby hand in Florence's long, knotty hand, with its age spots. Forgive me, my dear. I must have heard your message, I always listen to my messages, at least once a week – a smile – but sometimes I forget to write them down, and then I end up forgetting them. She tapped on her temple with her index finger. I'm a little absent-minded, she said.

And when we walked in and met Norbert, who then left with his vacuum cleaner, she suggested that we have a seat and went to get the tea. She brought a blue teapot and a collection of mismatched cups. All made by her, she announced. Here she had used melted glass. This one here was already quite old, one of the first cups she had made when she was still living and studying in Mexico. Then she looked at me and with a start I suddenly wondered if she had met my mother. Did my mother's relationship with this woman's son include family gatherings? If so, how long would it take for her to recognize my mother in me?

Sugar, anyone? Honey?

Then she talked, with her eyes wandering through the air, about when she was young and lived in Mexico and met her first husband and then they both went to live in the Ivory Coast, and his name was Jesus. Her first husband. A good man. Her two children had been born in Abidjan. And after living in Mexico and the Ivory Coast she had never again been able to live in a cold climate.

In Vermont with Norbert, for example, she said. It's all very beautiful there, but I need the sun. Norbert wanted me to move to Vermont when we met. I said no. I told him he had to choose. Vermont or me.

Carlos had gotten up and gone to play with the cat. I asked its name and Florence said Salmon, and Carlos thought it was funny for a cat to have a fish name.

So where are your kids these days?

It was Fernando who asked the question, and only I knew that his voice was shaking on the inside, under his mantle of casualness and politeness. Only I knew that his voice was a trap. Three pairs of eyes trained themselves on Florence, trying not to look anxious.

They've gone back to Africa. My son's been in Abidjan for six years now. My daughter's been in Luanda for more than ten. Her husband is from there. Would anyone like some more tea? Have some ginger cookies. I made them yesterday.

How stupid, I thought. How stupid to leave Copacabana and go live in a suburb of Denver and wait months and travel hundreds of miles in a crappy old car to find a woman in a house tucked away in the mountains of New Mexico only to discover that my father lived in Africa. That he was a whole Atlantic away. That he was on a continent which, outside of the classroom, I had rarely thought about in my thirteen years of life, on a continent that had nothing to do with me or my mother, or Barra do Jucu, or Janis Joplin.

I was phenomenally angry at myself for the idea, for the letter, I was angry at the post office employee for having sent the letter properly and at the letter for not having gotten lost in the post, I was angry at Fernando for the nice little phone call, I was angry at Carlos for existing and having that stupid family of his and for not being able to speak English properly after a year in the country that he and his stupid family worshipped, I was angry at Florence for the triviality of her words and her la-la land, and for having a husband who collected vacuum cleaners. I was angry at the tea. I was angry at the Indians and their jewelry in Santa Fé and at the women who bought the Indians' jewelry in Santa Fé and even more at their rich, potbellied husbands. I was genuinely abysmally angry at the librarian at the Denver Public Library, who had suggested all that poetry to me as if I had some kind of aspiration to become an intellectual. As if anyone needed it. That pile of difficult lines written by men and women who didn't have anything else to do. I was angry at WH, TS and WB, and very angry at Marianne and her dumb fish. I was angry at my mother for dying and at myself for having been left behind, for staying on in my compulsory life, unable to escape the teachers' pity and my classmates' teary eyes. I felt a compact, vehement anger for playing on the ultimate team and being Aditi Ramagiri's friend and having Nick's name written on my jeans. I was angry at Shah Jahan and his damned missing diamond.

I felt like screaming. Like picking up the teacup and smashing it against the white wall. A new Big Bang that wouldn't beget any universes – just a handful of ceramic fragments that someone would sweep into a dustpan. A Big Bang without universal pretensions, like an outlet for a god's bad mood.

But I didn't scream or throw the teacup. I remained silent, as Florence delivered a slow monologue like someone remembering a dream, talking about her work, her sculptures, her pottery, and suggested that we go and see the sculptures in the garden while it was still light out, and then she would show us her studio. Lots of things were for sale and she accepted cash or checks, but not credit cards unfortunately.

Fernando held my hand as we headed out into the garden and sparse snowflakes twirled in the white sky, undecided as to their destination. The weather disobeyed meteorology. But the snowflakes disappeared on the ground. They didn't come to be presences.

Fernando held my hand with a squeeze that wasn't loose or tight, and as we walked around the garden and looked at the Woman Chicken and other sculptures we wondered, all of us, each in the dialect of our own thoughts, how we would tell Florence the real reason for our visit. And whether she would be upset or happy or suspicious, or none of the above.

Probably none of the above.

It was already night when we left the house on Redondo Road. June got into her green pickup and placed the half-dozen ceramic tea cups she had bought, wrapped in several sheets of newspaper and stacked in a plastic bag, on the passenger seat next to her.

June would take the same route back to Santa Fé, where Alfred and Georgia were waiting for her, perhaps already a little upset at her long absence. She would pass through Los Alamos and cross Oppenheimer Drive; she would pass the Indians' brightly lit casinos and neon signs.

Fernando, Carlos and I would continue south after leaving
Redondo Road, along the modest State Road 4. We would pass
through Jemez Pueblo and reach San Ysidro, where the road
emptied into another, and we would pass through Zia Pueblo and
continue on to the intersection of I-25, the omnipresent Interstate
25. And we would see other Indians' brightly lit casinos and neon
signs. And at some point we would be in Albuquerque. I was holding a two-dimensional ceramic creature. A lizard, perhaps. A creature made by Florence.

I don't sell these ones. I make them as a pastime, she had said.
Pick one.

Florence's studio was a large room with a really big dirty table
and pieces of newspaper everywhere. But she hadn't hung her
favorite poem on the wall. Maybe she didn't have a favorite poem.
Maybe she didn't read poems.

I picked the perhaps-lizard. Which was now arriving in
Albuquerque with me – the same Albuquerque where I had been
born and which I was revisiting with a strange reverence, the reverence reserved for reencounters with people and places we don't
remember anymore.

Anaconda

ON FRIDAYS, MY mother used to get her nails done and would come home complaining about the smell of the nail polish. On Saturdays, she used to go to the street market and would come home complaining about the smell of the fish. On Tuesdays, she used to go to the supermarket and would come home complaining about the price of things.

Sometimes I would go with her to the manicurist and the manicurist would paint my nails pink. I didn't complain about the smell of the nail polish.

After my mother died, I wondered if all these places would save her a space for a while. The space that she would have occupied in the queue at the supermarket. The lettuce or the potatoes that she would have bought at the street market. The potential brushstrokes of nail polish in the bottle. I wondered if the space that a person occupies in the world survives the person themself. If the stage remains set for a while, the props ready, the cue repeated several times, waiting for the person to come on again. And if the connections are only undone slowly, the threads breaking, the lights switching off, the person dying slowly for the world after they have died for themself. If there are two deaths, one intimate and individual, the other public and collective, two deaths that happen at different paces.

Perhaps Fernando had heard, before me and somewhere else, my mother complaining about the smell of the nail polish, the smell of the fish and the price of things. Perhaps she had scolded him about leaving coffee cups around the house and perhaps he had scolded her for forgetting to give him a message. Perhaps they had both woken up several mornings not speaking to one another. Perhaps he had placed his finger lightly on Suzana's neck to feel the blood pulsing there. Perhaps she had traced his eyebrows with her fingertips.

One day he told her about the past. About weapons. About Brasilia, Peking, the River of the Macaws. One day she told him about the past. About the lamb in the song. About her mother's dolls. About the dead cat sprawled across the sidewalk.

One day she told him about her father and Texas, but only some of it. One day he told her about the girl he had met on the banks of the Araguaia, but only some of it. She told him that she had severed ties with her father and moved to the next state. Without a penny to her name. He told her that he had been fond of the girl who had fought beside him in the guerrilla war. Fernando knew how to make weapons. Suzana knew how to leave men. Fernando had studied at the Peking Military Academy. Suzana had donated her mother's dolls to a Presbyterian orphanage in Dallas. Fernando had a letter from his guerrilla girlfriend, which he had kept almost by accident. Suzana had a photo of her mother. And one day they had lain down in bed with their memories, their ghosts, their deaths.

Do you promise? asked Suzana before she fell asleep.

Promise what? he asked.

Promise first and I'll tell you afterwards.

I promise.

And she looked at the digital clock on the bedside table and saw that it was the next day.

Now tell me what I promised, said Fernando.

But she didn't. She allowed her head to sink between two pillows and closed her burrow with the blanket and snuggled into sleep, into the happiness of sleep, into the inconsequence of sleep. And since Fernando never found out what he had promised, he had to improvise the keeping of the promise.

For this reason, and this reason alone, he stayed on in the United States when he and my mother broke up, a state's distance away, where he could get in his car and drive for six hours to, for example, register as his daughter the daughter who wasn't his. For this reason he was there every time she called him and left every time she asked him to. For this reason: for her.

And when she returned to Brazil he stayed put, according to the promise he had improvised and, improvising, kept.

He stayed put, like a property, a house, something that you don't uproot and cart about, in your pocket, your suitcase, your back-pack. A structure built on the earth, heavy, sealed, protected from the weather, prepared for the extreme cold and the extreme heat, capable of closing doors and windows to the wind, capable of closing curtains to the eyes of passersby.

In case she decided to return some day.

And every day that she didn't decide to return was added to the previous day like a calendar that you put together yourself, to which you add pages, and suddenly he took it all and stashed it in the wooden El Coto de Rioja wine crate and put it at the back of the wardrobe and thought it no longer made any difference. Staying, leaving. It wasn't an issue anymore.

Someone mentioned a position as a security guard at Denver Public Library, right in the center of town, that clean, airy, functional place where books were shelved, catalogued, where people went like informal pilgrims to consult or borrow the books. A security guard at a library felt like something of a formality to him. A position in the world that was mere protocol. He figured that libraries weren't violent places, requiring security. He couldn't imagine library-goers being thieves or attackers or troublemakers.

At the entrance was an inscription with the words of Jorge Luis Borges: *I have always imagined Paradise as a kind of library.* There should be no need for security guards in a place with such a paradisiacal statute.

But you never know.

The job was there. And Fernando was there to try and get the job.

Years later, as the red 1985 Saab convalesced in a mechanic's workshop near Starkville, in Las Animas Country, almost on the

Colorado-New Mexico border, Fernando asked me: do you want me to tell you the things I never told your mother?

I was quiet and listened. For a good while, I just listened. I never asked Fernando why he decided to talk that night. If he had decided to indemnify my mother for the things he hadn't told her by telling her daughter.

Whatever his reason, the story that hadn't been told started on the first anniversary of the Araguaia Guerrilla Movement.

The anaconda is the second-largest snake in the world. In the Amazon, it can reach twenty-six feet in length. People are afraid of the anaconda, but it avoids human beings. Most of the time.

Anaconda was the name of the operation that the army initiated in April of 1973. It was a plan to gather intelligence. Its objective wasn't to launch offensives against the enemy, but espionage, using the same methods to infiltrate the population as the guerrillas had used.

In the three preceding months, the dictatorship had killed four members of the Brazilian Communist Party's Central Committee in the cities. The dismantling of the party prevented new guerrilla reinforcements from being sent to the region.

Nevertheless, the atmosphere among the guerrillas was one of euphoria, and they wanted to believe that the inhabitants of the region would join the armed struggle. Their work with the local population continued. After several months, the guerrillas' Military Commission managed to re-establish contact with Detachment C, the most deeply affected by Operation Parrot. After some restructuring and under the orders of a new commander, Detachment C, in its first raid on property, occupied the farm of a land-grabber and government informer. They confiscated a sum equal to that which the farmer had obtained selling the guerrillas' possessions after one of their camps had been occupied by the army.

The threat of reprisal spread among the locals who had betrayed the guerrillas. One such local, Pedro Mineiro, was executed in his own home, after being judged by the Revolutionary Military Tribunal. Another peasant by the name of Osmar was also captured, judged and executed.

For a while, Chico's hopes were renewed. It was hard not to take heart amidst the celebrations of the armed movement's first anniversary. The locals helped out with clothes, shoes, food. They listened to Tirana Radio with the guerrillas, attended meetings, and eleven of them ended up joining the cause.

But the fear that you once felt is a vaccine in reverse: it predisposes you to illness. It waits, in ambush. Like an anaconda ready to devour its prey, ready to wrap around it and drag it to the river or, with scientific precision, squeeze it a little more every time it exhales, until it is no longer possible for it to fill its lungs with air. The anaconda has no venom. Its weapon is oppression.

In Operation Anaconda, there were explicit orders for there to be no military action. Unless they were lucky enough to find Osvaldão, the black giant who commanded Detachment B. The ophidian information network in the Araguaia region turned captains, lieutenants, soldiers and sergeants into rural workers, malaria control sprayers, tavern-goers, Land Reform Agency inspectors, traveling salesmen. But it wasn't easy. The operation that should have taken two months took five.

★   ★   ★

In September, a group of guerrillas from Detachment A arrived at daybreak at a Military Police post on the Trans-Amazonian Highway. They surrounded it. After shouting for the soldiers to surrender, which they didn't, the detachment commander ordered the guerrillas to open fire. The post went up in flames. The soldiers came out and surrendered. After being interrogated in their underwear and threatened with execution, they were evicted. The loot taken by the guerrillas included weapons, ammunition, uniforms and boots, and their success was recounted in a communiqué to the inhabitants of the region.

Manuela was among the guerrillas who took part in the operation. Chico should have been.

But there was a moment, before daybreak, as the Araguaia communists were heading for what was to be their first successful military offensive, when Chico stopped. The others continued on, believing in their feet and hands and eyes and weapons, and Chico stopped.

No one saw him. The sky was still dark in a winter that had barely ended, in the heart of a forest that Trans-Amazonian Highways bled awkwardly, without talent, without conviction. Somewhat embarrassed, knowing perhaps that they would never be more than sketches of highways.

Chico thought about Peking. He thought about the opera, and the painted masks on the faces of the singer-actors. He thought about their difficult voices, which made curves that were different to those of the singers he knew. He thought about his Chinese interpreters, and the many nights and many days he had spent in that faraway country, then he thought no more.

He saw Manuela in the distance, from behind, her hair tied back, the hair that had once belonged to a Rio student versed in language and literature, nail polish and special shampoos and who was now versed in hoes, knives and guns. She was much thinner than when she had arrived here, that rainy day, yet another rainy day. Beneath her dry skin covered in sores were new muscles for new skills. And Chico thought about how people's bodies were adaptable: to cold, to heat, to fear, to hunger, to work. To hoes, knives and guns.

He saw Manuela in the distance and it was the last time he saw Manuela.

She kept going and he stayed were he was. He could have taken a step, and it would have been the first of many more, as he accompanied the group headed for the Military Police post. All he had to do was lift up his foot and put it down a little further away; it was a step and didn't require training or philosophy and he'd known how to do it since he was a child. Communist guerrillas took steps, dictators took steps, men and women and old people and children in Brazil, in China, in Albania, in the United States, in Cuba and in Bolivia and even on the moon took steps. But he stayed where he was for a time which was a potholed asphalt road slicing through his life from east to west. From the Atlantic to the Peruvian border. And the longer he stood there, Chico knew, an unforeseen decision was being sealed – unforeseen and, in the pit of his stomach, more shameful than the military's shameful inability to do away with that group which, for any number of reasons, should have been exterminated a long time ago. They, the guerrillas, were ghosts walking through the forest, believing (believing?) in another world. They were already ghosts. If he had gotten close to Manuela again, he might have seen through her skin. She was possibly already losing ownership of her body, as it was obvious that she would, sooner or later. Like him. Like all of them.

Chico never got close to Manuela again. Being the skillful woodsman that he was, he found his way out of there, far from there, far from everything, himself included.

The killing would begin the following month. The hunt for the guerrillas and the extermination of all of them. The military would pick them off one by one. Perhaps Chico sensed it. Perhaps he only suspected it. Feared it. Gave up.

Chico didn't hear the detachment commander's shouts that morning. He didn't see the soldiers coming out of the post amidst flames and smoke. He didn't see them being evicted. Chico didn't see Manuela looking for him, the rest of the detachment too but especially Manuela, looking for him. Manuela, who had been his companion during such a troubled time, and who would be one of the missing of the Araguaia Guerrilla Movement, a presumed pile of bones among the presumed piles of bones buried in unknown places, a question mark in the official history of the country in the decades to come. How could Chico have imagined it all? Chico never had news of her again – and it was with a bitter aftertaste that he heard that love song, when he heard it. *Como é que você não me diz quando é que você me faz feliz? Onde é que vamos morar?* (Why won't you tell me when you are going to make me happy? Where are we going to live?) It was with a bitter aftertaste that he harbored his certainty of her uncertainty: Had Chico been captured? Killed?

Had he deserted? (No, Chico wouldn't have deserted. Chico wasn't the sort. He had been to the Peking Military Academy. He was good with weapons. And other things.)

Chico made a quick stopover in Goiânia. He said goodbye to his mother and left. He never set foot in Brazil again. Six months later he was serving draft beers in a London pub, and singing out loud when he felt like it, and off-key if he had to.

Vista del Mundo

JUNE HAD SAID that we should look up Isabel in Albuquerque. There was a time when my mother's house on San Pablo Street became a confluence of worlds, friends of diverse origins, Spanish students, English students, Portuguese students, with Spanglish reverberating within the walls of the 1950s house – vintage, they would say today – as music by Noel Rosa and Milton Nascimento played in the background. My mother would have been the owner of a vintage house, promoted to the "charming" category by the passage of time. Without her having gone to any effort, without her having paid for the privilege. June used to visit my mother's house sometimes, back then, with her Queen's English and her royal consort. According to June, Isabel also used to frequent my mother's house. They held parties almost daily.

Not long before you were born, June explained. Isabel was Suzana's English student. They ended up becoming friends. Isabel had recently arrived from Puerto Rico and was studying theatre. And she knew how to make mojitos and margueritas.

So she's an actress?

No, said June.

And she didn't say anything else. The things June didn't say were another kind of chatter. If she suddenly went vehemently quiet, there was no room for you to ask her a thing.

Later Isabel went back to Puerto Rico for a few years, she went on. But she's been back in Albuquerque for a while now and would love to meet you. All of you.

We spent the night in a motel chosen for its price. Carlos decreed that it was *muy bueno*. Very good. The heated pool was a little bigger than the one at the motel near Starkville, and the towels were whiter. The bedroom was better lit, the bedspreads newer and the watercolors on the walls less faded.

That night we didn't talk. Fernando turned on the TV, selected a Mexican channel and watched a soccer game and Carlos wrote down the Highlights of the Day in a notebook that Florence had given him as a present. In his shaky scrawl, he wrote the motel in Albuquerque is very good. And he showed me, pleased with himself. He had brought some more tourist brochures from the reception and read to me that Albuquerque had OVER THREE HUNDRED YEARS OF HISTORY. He asked if we could buy some scissors and glue the next day, because he wanted to cut those things out and stick them in his notebook.

I looked at the brochure. *The Albuquerque area was inhabited by Native Americans for hundreds of years. The current city was founded in 1706, when Governor Francisco Cuervo y Valdez wrote a letter to the*

Duke of Albuquerque telling him that he had found a village on the banks of the Rio Grande. From that time on, the city – named after the duke – grew from a small settlement into a wealthy metropolis with over eight hundred thousand inhabitants. Come visit the city where the people and culture are

Fernando?

What?

What's this word here?

He glanced at the brochure. Enmeshed.

What does enmeshed mean?

Imagine a net, a mesh. If something's enmeshed it's like it's caught in a net. Tangled.

And he demonstrated by interlacing the fingers of both hands, without taking his eyes off the television.

Enmeshed was a funny word. I tested it in my mouth, in a whisper. *Come visit the city where the people and culture are enmeshed in the fabric of time and history.*

I thought about it. Was it possible for the people and culture of a place not to be enmeshed in the fabric of time and history? Was there a people or a culture without time or history? But it was just a tourist brochure and tourist brochures, I was learning, hadn't been written to make sense. The words had to be pretty. So did the photos. The photos in the tourist brochure of Albuquerque were pretty and showed a bunch of dry chilies hanging from a veranda, a couple riding bicycles on a mountain trail (their helmets didn't have rear-view mirrors), and a lot of hot air balloons in the blue sky of the HOT AIR BALLOONING CAPITAL OF THE WORLD.

Carlos finished writing what he needed to write in his note-book, put his brochures away, turned off the bedside lamp and fell asleep with his head on my shoulder. I closed my eyes. I drifted off, lulled by the low volume of the TV on which a Mexican sports commentator was narrating the plays of the game so fast I couldn't keep up. Before my eyes closed, I saw the walls changing colors.

Fernando held my hand as we walked around Florence's dry garden and looked at the sculptures without paying attention. It was the only time that he and I walked along holding hands. He held my cold little hand with his cold large hand and at a glance, genetics aside, we could have been father and daughter.

Then we entered Florence's studio and there was the spirit of things in progress there. The studio was a place in the gerund, a place where things left their crude state, being produced, becom-ing. Florence kept the pottery that she sold in a large cupboard with glass doors and invited us to have a look and gave me and Carlos a lump of clay each.

For you to make something with. Anything at all.

Carlos stared seriously at the misshapen lump of clay in his hand, creased his forehead and started kneading and tugging on it to see if maybe something would come out of there of its own accord. A spontaneous sculpture. I took my piece and started rolling it in my hands. All my creativity was able to produce, at that moment, was a ball. Something disobliged to have angles, a round artifact. A globe of earth.

Florence?

Yes?

It was June who had spoken. Florence, she repeated, we need to talk to you.

Talk? Florence smiled and shook her head a little and her hair shook on her head. OK, let's talk.

And she pulled up a chair and June and Fernando sat on a couch covered with an old wool blanket. Carlos and I remained standing, a slight distance away, playing with the lumps of clay in our hands. Florence sat on the chair, her body leaning slightly forward, hands in her lap with her fingers interlaced.

Your work is very beautiful, June continued, appointing herself spokeswoman of the group, and cleared her throat. Very beautiful. But that's not why we came here.

Florence was listening, very attentive and interested, as if we were about to give her a far-reaching explanation of the butterfly effect or antimatter.

We came here because of that little girl over there.

The faces all turned towards me and I, not knowing what to do, did nothing and kept rolling my ball of clay.

Some time ago, in the late seventies, Vanja's mother came to live in New Mexico, June continued. She was quite young. Her name was Suzana. She had come here from Brazil when she was still a child, with her father, after her mother died.

June spoke slowly. With her smile fading slightly at the lack of sense in those words, Florence listened.

Some time later, a few years later, Suzana married Fernando (and June placed her hand on his shoulder, but quickly removed it, as if she had committed an indiscretion, a faux pas). And later they broke up. And she had a short relationship with another man. Your son Daniel. It didn't last long. I don't know if you ever met her. Probably not.

Florence was beginning to understand. She showed it by nodding. A relationship with her son Daniel. Short. Didn't last long.

When was that? she asked.

They spent some time together in early 1988, said Fernando. It's been almost fourteen years. She lived in Albuquerque, on San Pablo Street Northeast.

I was surprised by Fernando's instant math. But maybe he knew those numbers off by heart. Maybe he knew that (other) story off by heart, a compulsory talent he wished he didn't have.

Yes, said Florence, Daniel lived in Albuquerque at that time. But I only remember meeting one girlfriend of his, from his time in Albuquerque, and she wasn't called Suzana. She was Ashley. Or Audrey. Or Abigail. Something like that, that started with an A. It's been a long time.

Florence understood, but she didn't understand everything.

We came here, June continued, because during the time she spent with your son Suzana fell pregnant, and at the end of the year she had a daughter.

And everyone looked again *at that little girl over there*, life model, guinea pig, a bizarre specimen with some deformity or shocking dysfunction visible to whoever went to the trouble of looking.

The obvious question, that I (dysfunctional) had never thought of: what guarantee was there that I really was the daughter of that woman's son? One could only be sure of such things by resorting to the cold protocol of science. What guarantee was there that that whole story – Suzana, Albuquerque, short relationships – was true? We might have been a bizarre troupe of experimental con artists, trying to see if we could convince innocent old ladies with our heterogeneous accents and cock-and-bull stories involving dubious paternities and abnormal disappearances.

But she got up and came over to me. She gazed into my eyes. She forgot whatever it was that usually danced in the aerial space just over her forehead. She forgot Fernando, June and Carlos.

Is it true? she asked me.

Of course Florence was looking for Daniel in me. And I wondered if I too would have seen him in my passport photo if I had known him, if I would have reencountered him in the genetic amalgam of my face, or if my mother didn't need men even for that. Not even to lend a little of their biotype to her daughter. I wondered what Florence was seeing there in her trance, as she stared at that speechless thirteen-year-old oracle, rolling a ball of clay in her hands.

And I felt strange. I, who had always refused impossible projects (like the horizon seen from Copacabana), had devoted myself to one that was almost that: a fairytale father, a father scattered across the globe by myself in a number of potential places – all of them beyond the horizon seen from Copacabana. Of course: among all of the potential places I hadn't listed the Ivory Coast. And yet there was less ocean and sky between Rio de Janeiro and the Ivory Coast than between Rio de Janeiro and the western United States.

If I set sail by boat from Copacabana, all I'd have to do was travel straight in a northeasterly direction to arrive at the Ivory Coast. If

I arrived very secretively, a smuggler of myself, I wouldn't even need a passport, I wouldn't even need to stop at an immigration official's booth and go through the tedious border protocol.

It didn't really matter if this woman believed me (us) or not. She could shoo us out of there and tell us never to come back, opportunists that we were. And I would shrug as effortlessly as Fernando did, his habitual effortlessness. And I would leave there and never return and she could think what she wanted of me (us). I felt as if I'd entered the wrong movie theater and instead of finding an exciting science fiction film I'd come across a romantic comedy or a musical. I hate musicals. I definitely didn't know what I was doing there anymore: in Florence's studio, on Redondo Road, in Jemez Springs, in New Mexico, in the United States, in the northern hemisphere; I didn't even know what I was doing on the third ball orbiting the sun. Everything was strange and I felt strange with that woman staring at me through her milky eyeballs.

And she stared and stared and kept staring. Until she found what she was looking for.

When I woke up in the motel in Albuquerque, I was alone. There was a note in Carlos's handwriting in Portuguese (dictated, of course) on the bedside table. WE'VE GONE TO BRAEKFAST. WE DIDNT WANT TO WAKE YOU. WE'LL BRING A BAGEL. I had gone to bed with wet hair (where was my mother to tell me I shouldn't do that? In what recess of my memory?) and an egg of hair had appeared on the right side of my head. I wet it in the sink. I combed it. It made no difference. I forgot about it and went out to find Fernando and Carlos.

They were eating breakfast in silence, staring at the huge TV on the wall in front of a group of squalid little tables. A politician was talking about politics on the TV.

You've got an egg on your head, said Fernando. Carlos laughed.

We drove around Albuquerque ceremoniously. Fernando was quieter than usual. Carlos jotted down the names of streets and any information that struck him as relevant in his notebook. We went to San Pablo Street Northeast and I was dismayed to discover that I remembered nothing of the house where I had spent the first two years of my life. Nothing. Zero.

It was like a slice of earth that had been removed from the ground. It had a dry garden in front of it just like Florence's dry garden, but smaller. It had a dry tree. We got out of the car and wandered down the block aimlessly. It wasn't as cold there but it was still cold and I pulled my stocking hat (which I'd put on to cure my messy hair) down over my ears.

There wasn't the slightest recognition in me. Fernando could have been telling me a big lie, showing me a house chosen at random, and it wouldn't have made any difference.

But there was recognition in him and it wasn't easy and I knew it.

Did houses purge themselves of their former inhabitants with the arrival of their new inhabitants? Or were there several layers of ghosts in their memories, like layers of wallpaper? Did houses have memories?

Even if they didn't, adult men did. Fernando had lived in that house with my mother for six years. Fernando had slept in that house with my mother for six years, and woken up, and looked at the dry tree when it was dry in the winter and when it was green in the summer and in all of its in-between stages. He had walked through those rooms for two thousand days. He had opened the door as he got home from work (which made me realize that I didn't know what his job had been). He had closed the door as he left for work. And one day he had closed the door for the last time and it hadn't been as he left for work.

Do you want to take a photo? Fernando asked.

I said yes and he took his old camera out of his jacket pocket and told Carlos and me to stand in front of the house (when we got the film developed, we would see that I had my eyes closed and Carlos's mouth was a bit crooked, because he was about to say something or run his tongue over his parched lips).

Then we went back to the car and I considered the expedition to my early childhood over.

There wasn't much else to do besides leave. Put those events in our pockets and leave. Celebrate Thanksgiving with June and her senile dogs the next day, and spend the two days after the next day at her place on Camino Sin Nombre, and scale the map again with our noses pointing north and the hope that the Saab wouldn't decide to break down again.

Yes, of course, there were the Next Steps, and they were frighteningly toilsome. I searched my soul for energy, determination, courage, patience and other honorable sentiments. Other military-salute sentiments, the sort that make up the marrow of heroes.

But the next day and the day after that and the day after that still had something to say, before the rest of my once-again-post-New-Mexican life could begin. There was still, at least, a localizable vestige of my mother in Albuquerque, and that vestige was called Isabel and we were going to meet her.

Isabel appeared in a white kimono, the kind used by people who practise martial arts, tied with a green belt. I didn't know if it put her down at the bottom of the hierarchy, up at the top or somewhere just so-so. Over it she was wearing a waterproof jacket that was very thick and very green.

She walked into the coffee shop where we had arranged to meet, picked her way through the people until she got to our table and hugged me. We were almost the same height. Then she shook Fernando's hand with martial-arts vigor and Carlos's hand with the same martial-arts vigor.

She sat down and looked at the enormous slice of chocolate cake that Carlos was eating and asked what's that? Can I have a taste? And Carlos cut a (small) piece off with his fork and held it up to her mouth and thought it was funny. Him, a boy, feeding a grown woman. There was chocolate with chocolate filling and chocolate icing and pieces of chocolate negligently smeared around the Salvadorian boy's mouth, but they disappeared politely into the Puerto Rican woman's mouth.

And she said I'm always starving after practice.

And Carlos asked if she did judo or karate and she said aikido. And he said he'd never heard of it. And she said I'll take you down later so you can see what it's like.

We chatted. She and Fernando had two cups of coffee each. His without sugar. Hers with a full spoonful. We talked about places: Rio de Janeiro, Albuquerque, Colorado, Puerto Rico. We talked about people: me, my mother, my foster aunt, Carlos (we didn't talk about Fernando).

Do you want to be an actress? I asked at some point.

I used to, she said. Before. But it didn't end up happening.

But you studied theatre. June told us.

For a while. I came here to go to college.

So if you're not an actress, what are you?

And she held her palms up and tilted her head to one side in a pantomime gesture.

I'm not anything.

But Carlos exclaimed, from his podium, that she did aikido (even though he didn't know what aikido was, but it sounded Japanese and serious). A person who does aikido and wears aikido clothes can't not be anything – was his argument.

And she laughed and said I'd like to have you all over for dinner at my place. Can you come? I bought some things that we used to make at your mother's place – at your place (and she turned to me and then to Fernando, who could claim that possessive adjective to different degrees and for different reasons). For old times' sake.

The old times were just that, old times. Times gone, past, yester-year, a long time ago. Back when the "in" thing was for Isabel and my mother's friends to get together in the house on San Pablo Street, when Fernando wasn't part of Suzana's life anymore and I had yet to be. So the old times were also pages from another calen-dar – and I thought again about what Pope Gregory had taken (I confess that I was kind of obsessed with the story: the omnipo-tence of a man of the cloth who stole time).

But we were there, we were with Isabel and having dinner with her seemed to be an imperative of the new times, more than an homage to the old. And at any rate she was enchanting. And at any rate we didn't have anything else to do.

We followed her car from the coffee shop in Nob Hill to the suburb of Vista del Mundo, where she lived, in an enormous house that was one hundred percent contrary to anything that I might have imagined for her and her aikido clothes and green belt and green jacket, and her thin wrists and thick hair. It was enormous and looked a lot like the confectioner's houses I had seen in Denver's wealthy suburbs. It was a placid color in an undefined pastel tone and there was a cypress on each side of the door, like little green soldiers with conical bodies.

Isabel made mojitos for Fernando and herself and I noticed his relief at having the glass to put his hand on, and the rum to sip. It hadn't been an easy day.

You live in a very big house, he said – and perhaps added mentally: for someone who isn't anything.

It's not mine.

And she went over to the sound system to put on some music. I couldn't understand why adults only half-answered so many things. Maybe it was a mature, civilized habit and I should just get used to it. I was going to turn fourteen the following month. Fourteen was at least a nose in the adult world. And I had to unlearn all the codes I had learned to make way for others. Curiosity, for example: children had a gift for curiosity. Adults kept it chained up. In adults, curiosity shook paws, fetched balls and played dead.

I looked around at that house that was bigger than Isabel. Everything was more than necessary, as she appeared to live alone.

There was too much floor, too many windows, too much furniture for just one person.

We would have dined in Vista del Mundo with Isabel, who had gone upstairs to her room and come back ten minutes later in civilian clothes with wet hair, hair that was very curly and hung in the air exactly like the questions that we all wanted to ask about her life (present, past) but weren't sure if we should. And before the clock struck midnight we all would have been in our motel-room beds and Carlos would have written up every stage of the dinner at Isabel's place in his notebook, beginning, middle and end. And I would have bathed and also taken care to dry my hair better this time, and it's possible Fernando would have listened to Mexican soccer commentators on TV.

But Carlos and his chocolate cake were conspiring, in silence, in his stomach. They were planning a small guerrilla war. A mini-revolution.

He started complaining of nausea at 7.23pm after eating tortilla chips with guacamole. At 8.11pm, he started throwing up tortilla chips with guacamole (together with the chocolate cake, the main conspirator).

Because of those unruly, restless foods, and Carlos's stomach's desire to return them as one might return faulty merchandise, we ended up spending the night at Isabel's house. After midnight, after a febrile Carlos had vomited enough and gone to bed, and I had gone to bed too, to dream memories of houses that I didn't remember, I felt thirsty and got up, almost sleepwalking, to get a glass of water. The door of the next room, where Fernando should have been sleeping, was ajar. I glanced through the crack and even in the leaden half-light I could see that his bed was untouched and the room empty.

I wondered if maybe I shouldn't get that drink of water from the kitchen. I could have a drink from the bathroom sink, which was on the same floor as the bedroom. I was rather dubious as to what I might find in a house with doors ajar and men missing. But because my curiosity still wasn't a well-trained Labrador, I went downstairs anyway. Silently and slowly.

On the curve of the stairs, I craned my neck to peer into the living room and there they were, dancing to the sound of almost inaudible music, their bodies so close together that I felt embarrassed for seeing what I wasn't supposed to be seeing. And I went back to the bedroom before I could see anything else, like a kiss, like one of them sliding their hand down the other's back, like an opening in a blouse being explored by five fingers and a breast being found by those fingers. No, I didn't want to see any of that. And no, I didn't want to think about any of that either, but unfortunately thoughts are different: their freedom paralyzes ours. Thoughts do as they please.

WHAT FLORENCE DIDN'T FIND IN ME: 1) My father's eyes. They couldn't be found because, as I discovered later, he had blue eyes, and mine are brown. 2) Reasons not to believe me. As she was staring at me, I thought about mummies and how the ancient Egyptians used to remove the brains of their dead by stuffing hooks through their noses during the process of mummification. Perhaps she was trying, in those silent instants that lasted a few seconds that lasted a few decades, not to extract parts of me (courage? cheek?) for posterior embalmment but to appraise my trustworthiness using a method of her own. Which didn't involve hooks threaded through my nostrils, but two equally penetrating eyes and a prolonged absence of words. 3) The granddaughter she had always prayed for.

WHAT FLORENCE DID FIND IN ME: 1) The granddaughter she hadn't always prayed for – and surprises, in my opinion, have their charm. They're a kind of bonus. For example: you buy two packets of cookies in the supermarket and when you go to pay you discover that there's a special promotion that day: buy two packets of those cookies and get a packet of instant lemonade for free. 2) Some invisible, unspeakable merit which, faced with her two available options (putting me in contact with Daniel or not putting me in contact with Daniel), made her choose the former. 3) Something in my smile, a millimeter of curvature of my lips, that she would process over the following years until she told me one day, definitively: you have your father's smile.

Canis latrans

IT HAS BEEN said that coyotes, like crows, mediate between life and death and are common characters in mythology. They are extremely adaptable, omnivorous mammals and will eat almost anything available: rabbits, mice and squirrels, as well as birds, frogs and snakes, as well as insects and fruits, as well as carrion. In urban areas, the contents of trash cans and dog food. They have been known to attack domestic pets. In general, they hunt at night. In the wild, their average life span is six to eight years. They are found throughout Central America and most of North America, from Panama in the south as far as Canada and Alaska in the north. They sometimes starve to death, or fall victim to disease, or are caught in traps, or are killed by other animals, or are run over by cars. Some coyotes live alone, others in pairs, yet others in packs – which usually consist of a pair of adults, yearlings and cubs. Coyotes with a different scientific name smuggle illegal immigrants from Mexico into the United States.

In mythology, the coyote has the power of transformation. Sometimes it is a thief, as it is for the Hopi Indians. Sometimes it is the creator of humanity, as it is for the Navajos, or of the earth, as it is for the Miwoks. Sometimes it is the creator of death, as it is for the Chinook people: once upon a time Coyote and Water traveled to the world of the dead to bring their wives back, during an era in which death didn't exist for humans, only animals. As he was bringing the dead wives back in a box, however, Coyote couldn't help himself and opened it to see his wife. In so doing, he released the spirits of the dead and death itself. Which came to be a part of human life, so to speak.

When we returned to June's house in Santa Fé, after our two nights in Albuquerque, I saw the pair of coyotes in the dry river-bed. June came and got me in the middle of the night and took me to see them, from a distance.

In the dry riverbed there were also the carcasses of abandoned cars. Here and there, a kind of shy, seasonal junkyard. When the river came back to life, it would swell and the abandoned car carcasses would grow cold under the new water; another year, another river, the same river, a different river. Later the river would dry up again and they would be exposed once more, a little uglier, a little older, a little more carcass-like.

Over the years, my curiosity about Isabel's life was satisfied. Not that she had secrets. She was like my mother in that respect: she answered all questions. Except that, unlike my mother, she almost always said only what was necessary. She was rather martial and quiet. She came across as capable of beating up anyone who gave her a hard time in the street. But she never got into unnecessary arguments.

During the dinner at her place in Albuquerque, she told us part of her story. The second part. I pieced her life together from back to front, like someone following footsteps from their point of arrival to their point of departure.

So you live here alone? I asked, and if I was indiscreet it was too late, but everyone forgives children for that, and at the age of thirteen I was still in the comfortable position of being able to choose the situations in which I wanted to be considered a child and those in which I didn't, and to behave accordingly (there has to be some advantage in being thirteen).

Yes, she said, and the tortilla chips crackled in her mouth. But this house belongs to my ex-husband. He's got another one.

Another house?

Another house, another wife, another family.

In Albuquerque? Fernando asked, plucking up the courage.

In Seattle. He and his wife have a five-year-old boy.

How long have you been divorced?

Three years.

We were sitting at the table, four people at a table for eight, and I looked at the empty chairs, which looked like sad, speechless guests with lowered eyes. Half of the table was alive; the other half wasn't. Half of the table had plates, glasses, cutlery, tortilla chips; the other half didn't.

Three years, Fernando repeated.

Your math isn't wrong. My ex-husband always was a proactive kind of guy.

And just as Fernando was maybe about to apologize on his behalf and mine, for the overly Brazilian habit of wanting to know too many details about other people's lives, she let out a hearty, sincere cackle, and the three of us smiled and only then did Carlos ask what proactive meant.

It's like this, said Isabel. A guy who first chooses his new wife, then has a child with her, then gets a job and a house in another city, and only then leaves his old wife, is proactive.

Ah. I get it.

Carlos smiled, feeling smart for perceiving all the logic of that sequence. And it was an impeccable sequence. And logical.

Isabel smiled too, and I looked for traces of the bitterness that sometimes accompanies the jokes that adults make about themselves and didn't find any.

But the house isn't mine. One day I'm going to leave here, this house, this city. One day I think I'll go back to Puerto Rico. I'll go back again. The problem is that when I leave Puerto Rico I want to return, and when I return I want to leave again.

And Carlos said that he was going to return to El Salvador one day too, but just to visit, because now he was a Coloradoan. Or a Coloradan. Or whatever the name was. He was a non-native NATIVE. With mountains in the background.

I came here when I was eighteen, said Isabel. Then I went back to San Juan. Then I came back here again. I started working, met my husband, stopped working.

She shrugged.

I'm not proud of it. I'm thirty-four and what have I done with my life? Nothing. I live in his house, I live on the money he gives me. But I'm going to do something soon. I'm going to do something. Soon.

Be an actress? I asked.

And she looked at me with warmth in her eyes and crushed more tortilla chips with guacamole between her teeth.

Yeah, who knows? Maybe I'll be an actress.

Then she took the twig of mint out of her glass and ate it and said to Fernando I'm going to make another two mojitos. The food must be just about ready.

And when she got up and went into the kitchen Fernando turned his head and followed her with his eyes and I remembered the oh-so-common Rio character: the guy-looking-at-a-woman's-ass-as-she-goes-past. My mother used to say that we women should also look at men's asses as they go past. Which made me more comfortable about collating my penile statistics (left/right) at the beach. Although I would have done it anyway. But Fernando kept staring even after the ass and its owner and her long colorful skirt turned and stood in profile at the kitchen counter, and when they bent over to get mint leaves from the drawer in the refrigerator, and when the owner of the ass's arms scaled the top cupboard to get clean glasses and tossed the contents of the dirty glasses down the sink and turned on the garbage disposal, which went rrrrwmnwww, and stacked the dirty glasses in the dishwasher.

For a moment Fernando forgot that Carlos and I existed, and I looked at Carlos in search of solidarity. And that was when Carlos said he was feeling a bit weird. A bit nauseous.

After Operation Anaconda came Operation Marajoara. It started in October 1973. At first there were three hundred soldiers, all plainclothes, to fight what they estimated to be sixty-three guerrillas (the real number at that point was fifty-six).

In one week, Operation Marajoara had already reduced this number by four, all taken by surprise as they were preparing chunks of meat from two recently-slaughtered pigs. One of the men killed was the leader of Detachment A.

In its early days Operation Marajoara arrested a lot of locals, drove some crazy from the beatings they gave them, and set fire to houses and fields. People who refused to cooperate were punished. Sometimes they were placed head-down in barrels of water. Stuffed into one of those holes they used in Vietnam, with barbed wire over the top. Hung by their testicles.

The rainy season didn't intimidate the operation. It would continue throughout that October, and would see out the year on the Araguaia.

Soon afterwards another guerrilla, said to be very beautiful, was caught. She was shot in the leg first, and a soldier approached her and asked her name. And she said guerrillas don't have names, you bastard. I fight for freedom. And all of the soldiers in the patrol, almost ten of them, pumped the beautiful guerrilla full of bullets. Want freedom? There you go.

And soon after that another guerrilla was killed. He was found by his companions without his head – a trophy sent to the army base in Xambioá.

It became a fad and another combatant was decapitated after he was killed by soldiers.

★ ★ ★

Things weren't going so well for the communists. Several subsequent actions were unsuccessful. They still didn't have enough weapons or ammunition and many guerrillas no longer had any shoes. There were casualties and there were also deserters.

In the beginning the guerrillas had no idea of the size of the new military offensive. Little by little they learned. And that was how they spent Christmas of 1973, six years after they had moved into the region: listening to helicopters overhead. In other encounters with the forces of repression, throughout December, more of them were killed, including members of the guerrillas' Military Commission – and among them the commander general, Maurício Grabois, who went by the codename Mário.

Fernando, who was no longer Chico and was now far away, didn't know anything about it. He found out afterwards.

Afterwards he found out that the guerrillas who stayed in the area dispersed and then regrouped, trying to throw the enemy off their trail. But none of it did any good.

He also found out that a report from the Army Information Center, with the word SECRET (a word that was a hallmark of much of what went on in those days in that region, and would continue to be so for some time) stamped across the top said: *To Cease Operation "MARAJOARA" before the enemy has been completely destroyed could allow them to rise up again, with even greater vigor and experience. It could even provide them with proof of the viability, in BRAZIL, of guerrilla warfare in the countryside as an instrument in the struggle for power.*

In early 1974 a member of the guerrillas' Military Commission fled the forest – Ângelo Arroyo, Chico and Manuela's former commander at Detachment A. (He fled but insisted, back in São Paulo, that the armed struggle on the Araguaia should continue. Less than three years later, he was hunted down and murdered by the forces of repression.) Other members of the Central Committee, such as João Amazonas and Elza Monerat, hadn't been in the Bico do Papagaio region for quite some time.

In February, Osvaldão, another who had been there from the beginning, who was the communists' immortal warrior, was killed. His body was exhibited in local settlements. The immortal one was dead. Brought down by a woodsman. Then they made his body disappear. The military would finish exterminating the guerrillas with Operation Cleanup – a simple, crystal-clear, honest name that required no interpretation.

General Geisel, who took office that same month, said that the whole business of killing was regrettable, but it couldn't have been any different.

And with that the killings went on. And on. They needed to kill and then kill the deaths, so to speak. They needed to kill history. To kill the memory and a certain inconvenient awareness.

They all died, one by one. Some simply went missing, but missing was one of the codenames of death. It was another way to pronounce it.

Among the missing, among those who no one knew how they had died and where they were buried, was Manuela. She was captured one day when she went to visit a local woman who used to collaborate with the guerrillas, in search of food. Famished, thin, sick, barefoot, covered in sores and insect bites, Manuela spent the night at the woman's house and woke up surrounded by soldiers. That was the last anyone heard of her. Her parents grew old and died without ever knowing what happened to her.

The last guerrilla was executed in October. Walkíria Afonso Costa, a.k.a. Walk, was captured in Xambioá.

To erase their own footprints, the military decided to dig up the bodies, which were compromising, and burn them in the forest, which they did using tires and gasoline.

In the country's unofficial, confidential history, the Araguaia guerrilla war was over.

In São Paulo, Ângelo Arroyo continued to believe in the strategy of armed struggle in the countryside. In the second half of 1976, he traveled to other regions of the country in search of alternative scenarios for the fight. He visited the states of Rondônia, Acre and Mato Grosso, and sailed down the Amazon. He was machine-gunned down two days after the party's Central Committee met in São Paulo in December of that year, a meeting in which he continued to insist on the guerrilla movement.

Florence gazed at me. *We came here because during the time she spent with your son Suzana fell pregnant, and at the end of the year she had a daughter.*

Florence gazed at me as June, whose words still rang in the air, and Fernando, whose expectation resounded even higher, gazed at Florence and Carlos kneaded his ball of clay as if he were trying to pulverize it. To transmute earth into fireworks. To see dancing lights explode in the air and ricochet off sculptures and items of pottery.

Florence looked at me and asked, is it true?

I saw her eyes moving slowly within their orbits. I saw the wrinkles around her eyes growing longer and deeper, the genesis of a new mountain range in swift animation. Unstable plates were moving inside her, in a subterranean heart, amidst cold underground water and corridors of hot lava.

Why didn't you call me first?

We did, said June. A few weeks ago.

I must have heard your message – I listen to them at least once a week. But I'm a bit absent-minded. I think I've already told you that. And even if I didn't, you must have noticed. One notices such things.

It doesn't matter, said June.

No, said Florence. It doesn't.

And then, having obtained whatever it was that she needed, she turned to June and Fernando and said thank you for coming and for trusting me.

There was an inversion in that, I thought. She was the one who was trusting us. She was the one who was doing us the favor of believing, in a world of unbelievers and the mistrustful. She was the one who was accepting a tiny revision brought to her on a tray with tea and ginger cookies. A new member of the family on a plate, to use as a sugar substitute.

But Florence took my hands in hers, and it was as if our hands were also exchanging words, looks, completing phone calls that had gone astray. My small, thin, rough hands. Her long, knotty hands, with age spots.

★　★　★

Isabel came with us when we returned to June's house after that night in Vista del Mundo, in Albuquerque. I was going to celebrate Thanksgiving for the first time in my life, without really knowing what it was that we were celebrating, together with my Salvadorian friend, my mother's Brazilian ex-husband, my mother's old friend made-in-the-UK, my mother's former Puerto Rican student and the two old mastiffs. And the next day, now familiarized, we would look like a rehashed hippie community. And in the middle of the night I would see the pair of coyotes, the *Canis latrans*, which were thin, with long legs and pointy ears. The aloof, nocturnal pair.

On the Sunday, we would head back north. To Colorado, Lakewood and the house on Jay Street. Isabel would take a bus back to Albuquerque. And things would silently migrate out of themselves and become other things that no one imagined they would. Things would revolutionize themselves, slowly and quietly.

They say that the cells of your body are replaced every seven years, such that you continue to be the same person but, at a cellular level, you have become another, if you compute both extremes. The idea sounds strange, because the cells aren't all replaced at once, so after seven years you won't have a fully-recycled body. But at the same time you will.

Things I had hoped would happen didn't, things I hadn't hoped would happen did, and some things I'd never thought about – like visiting the Ivory Coast – thought about me of their own accord.

But in those days at June's house in Santa Fé we all laughed together and told stories about other times and other places, and sang songs from other times and other places (and from our time and our places) and looked at photographs. One morning we went to visit the Chimayo sanctuary, where the woman said *me puedes ayudar un dólar por favor* (I gave her the dollar and Fernando ignored her, asking in a low voice how I could fall for it but it was my money and my problem).

That night, as the coyotes roamed around outside, Fernando and Isabel disappeared into the room she was sleeping in, and no one asked any questions, and everyone thought it was fine. And we were so different to one another that the differences were annulled; we were a big uniformity in multiple forms.

On the Monday after the holiday, Fernando went to work at the Denver Public Library. I went to school. Carlos went to school.

That afternoon, Fernando had a cleaning job to go to.

Jay Street

WOULD FERNANDO HAVE liked Isabel to move to Colorado? I don't know. Would Isabel have liked to move to Colorado – or for Fernando to move to New Mexico, or to have moved with him to Puerto Rico or somewhere else in the world? I don't know.

None of it happened, because sometimes things are the wrong answers to the questions we ask, or the right answers to the questions we forget to ask. (There is no wisdom in this. It wasn't my grandmother who taught me – not least because I never met one of them, and I presented myself to the other one when I was almost fourteen years old and lacked the ears for teachings that she never seemed interested in passing on anyway.)

Perhaps neither Fernando nor Isabel suggested a move. Demonstrated their willingness. Like the water that you don't offer someone because you don't know they're thirsty, and the water that the thirsty person doesn't ask for because they don't want to impose, full of bourgeois ceremony. (Strange as it may seem, it was my mother who taught me that, adding: only be ashamed of things that are shameful, otherwise you're wasting your time. Shyness is unnecessary and boring.)

One day, years later, I visited June's house in Santa Fé once again. Her two dogs had died. She lived alone with her piano and her O'Keeffean skulls hanging on the walls. Coyotes roamed about outside. Perhaps they were the same ones. Or perhaps those ones had been run over or killed with a shotgun and other coyotes had come to replace them.

That day, June told me about Isabel.

She never did become an actress as she wanted, June said. But you saw how pretty she was. A little short, perhaps, but pretty. When she met her husband, she was working in one of those clubs, in Albuquerque, as a dancer. You know, taking her clothes off.

I didn't know.

That was where she met her husband, and he wanted her to stop working, and he bought that house, and married her, and you know the rest of the story.

Do you think she regrets it?

What?

Stopping working at the club.

She could have gone back.

I imagined (how not to?) Isabel dancing in the club in Albuquerque. Taking off her clothes, piece by piece, according to a deconstruction of decorum that hierarchically determined which piece had to come off first and which piece had to be last. The body twisting around itself and exposing itself in tiny doses, until it was entirely exposed (at which point the show ended, because the fun was in the process, otherwise she could have climbed up onto the stage buck naked). It must have been a sight. I'm not surprised that the guy who became her husband saw her there and wanted to take her home for free private sessions. That he wanted to rob the rest of humanity of the privilege.

I imagined him corroded with jealousy by Isabel's past, while she accepted naturally the fact that he had been and was still perhaps a frequenter of strip clubs. Was his new wife, up in Seattle, also an ex-stripper?

But for four nights Fernando had slept in the same bed with Isabel. For four nights he had sunk his rough fingers into her dark, wavy hair – her hair as dark as crow-blue shells and shell-blue crows – and had sunk his fingers into her hips, her dark hips, two big waves that were aligned with other waves that were aligned with other waves in wavy depths that at some point would arrive (would they?) at her essence. At her essence that was wavy, dark, blue, marine, ancestral like the Colorado sea and young like a young stripper dancing in a club in Albuquerque, the HOT AIR BALLOONING CAPITAL OF THE WORLD.

For four nights she had laughed with him in the same bed, slept with him in the same bed, lain awake with him in the same bed, sunk her fingers into his arms and his back and dreamed of a pair of coyotes outside and dreamed of a time when the Colorado sea covered it all and there were no coyotes wandering through Santa Fé because Santa Fé was underwater. Like the abandoned car carcasses when the river was full. She had dreamed of fish swimming through the windows of the future car carcasses in the future full river. She had dreamed of Mesozoic mollusks evolving at the bottom of the Colorado sea and dreamed in turn of future science museums. But maybe those were my dreams and Isabel's dreams on those nights were of the order of secrets, the unfathomable. Like the Mesozoic mollusks that vanished from the planet without a trace, a mark, a fossil, a message.

Maybe those four nights were enough and anything else was superfluous, and she and Fernando would have undone the magic of those four nights with the wand of routine if they had turned into four months or four years or multiples of that.

Maybe those four nights weren't enough but any philosophy of love involving impulsive sacrifices is one hundred percent stupid when put in practice. Saying certain things is beautiful. Living them out, not necessarily.

I know that Isabel and Fernando talked on the phone a few times. I also know that shortly after that long weekend she returned to Puerto Rico. She returned for good, as she had told us she might. She and Fernando talked on the phone a few times, until they stopped talking, like a noise that disappears into the distance and you don't know exactly when you stopped hearing it.

I turned fourteen that December. I turned fifteen twelve months later. And I turned other ages, sixteen, seventeen – the process follows an incredible logic. Eighteen. Etc.

I returned to Rio de Janeiro once, to visit Elisa. Things were the same and different. Seven years had passed since I had left and perhaps the city's cells had already been replaced with others. The city was the same and it wasn't. The city was different and it wasn't.

There were other generations of mollusks on the ocean floor in

front of Copacabana Beach. I don't know how long a mollusk
lives. They were probably the grandchildren and great grandchildren of the mollusks of my childhood. At any rate, we were friends.
Friends that had never met personally. Friends of friends, like in
online social networks.

There were young children building sandcastles in the sand.
There were their mothers. Depending on the place, tourists.
Depending on the place, prostitutes.

Bodies were still jogging in the sun, muscular or flaccid or old
or young. Men still wore tight speedos. Not all of them.

Fernando's house on Jay Street in Lakewood, Colorado, slowly
became my house too, by habit. By custom. By osmosis. We never
wondered if I'd leave or stay after all the Clarifications. I finished
the school year as a so-so student and entered the following school
year. And the next school year, which I also finished so-so, and
then the next. There was just one subject in which my grades were
honestly good and, at the end of the day, I had the Denver Public
Library librarian to thank for it. However, she wasn't present to get
teary-eyed and receive the applause of other teary-eyed people.
After I gave my thanks I felt kind of silly. Like a politician on an
election campaign, trying to say the nice things that people like to
hear. But it was already done. Every now and then I'd go swimming with Fernando, and we'd come home smelling of chlorine
and hang towels smelling of chlorine in the bathroom. One fine
day I realized that it didn't matter what country I was in. What city
I was in. Other things were important. Not these.

I never again forgot Fernando's birthday and the year after the
yellow T-shirt year Carlos and I bought him a bottle of Belgian

beer (with the help of a cooperative adult) and then, the next year, we bought him some perfume from Carlos's favorite store – a skateboarders' store, although he, Carlos, wasn't a skateboarder. Nor was he predestined to become one.

The winters became my winters and the summers my summers. So to speak. The in-between seasons stopped being a luxury and became, in the autumn, the rake that I use to rake up the leaves in front of the house and, in the spring, the flower that blooms in front of the house where I could have sworn nothing would survive the snow storms. And the flower blooms even if I don't look after the garden (I don't look after the garden). My customary, everyday things, like sleeping or cleaning my ears. When I learned to drive, I took Carlos to ride down the river in Boulder, with our backsides in tire tubes.

A little over a year ago I laid Fernando to rest. He died without guerrillas, wives or lovers. In his memory flowed rivers such as the Araguaia and the Thames and the cascading rivers in the mountains of Colorado, and the Rio Grande, which cuts through Albuquerque. But rivers find their way to the sea, and fresh waters become salty and peopled with sea creatures and their shells.

Fernando's body gave out one day as he was drinking coffee, during a break at work, and the whole thing went. His body spluttered like the motor of an old Saab, and it kept on spluttering, and then he started dying and continued dying until he was officially dead, which I was told by an Indian doctor with lowered eyes and tight, condolent lips.

I buried him, an ex-Fernando under the earth. And together with him, his ex-life and his ex-memories which, regardless of whether he shared them or not, would always be his alone and no one else's. Which he felt in the forest, which he felt in the London pub, which he felt sliding over the frozen mud in Peking. Which he felt when he embraced Manuela/Joana, Suzana, Isabel. Which he felt before and after those embraces. When he deserted these women or was deserted by them (*to desert: to leave empty or alone, abandon, withdraw from; to forsake one's duty or post with no intention of returning*). What he thought, what he planned and didn't do, what he promised and didn't deliver, what he did without any foreplanning, what he didn't hope for and got anyway.

A little over a year ago Carlos's parents moved to Florida, where Dolores, their disgraced runaway daughter, had become a prodigal daughter who kept twin cars with HIS (XO) and HERS (XO) license plates in her garage in Tallahassee. The sex of the cars causes a certain discomfort, I imagine, when Dolores's father and his moustache need to go out and only HERS is in the garage. Dolores's mother doesn't drive, so is spared any similar grief. But maybe the father has already bought himself a car with a regular license plate, with letters and numbers without meanings.

A little over a year ago Carlos crossed the street and came to live in this house, because he had promised never to leave Colorado or be far from me. So, while his parents got ready to move and sold furniture and bought one-way tickets to Florida, he got his things and transferred them here. He is a tall young man of eighteen. He still hasn't been back to El Salvador. Sometimes he asks to borrow my car and goes up into the mountains, like any native, intimate with the earth, the climate and its sharp changes, lamenting the avalanche that killed two unwary tourists (but who told them to go? You don't mess with the Rockies, he always says). I moved into the room that used to be Fernando's and Carlos moved into mine and with these minor migrations we stayed.

Nick, my schoolmate, kissed me once at a party. It felt weird for the first fifteen seconds, then it didn't. Our tongues got used to it, our teeth stopped being obstacles, and soon I wasn't thinking about tongues or teeth, but about other things with a sudden, desperate urgency.

The next year his family moved, he left the school, and at some point he must have reconsidered his political ideas because I heard recently that he'd become a marine.

At the same party where Nick kissed me, I was hanging a little earlier with a group of three girls from school, and at one point I went to straighten one girl's necklace and said I think it's better like that, and she said I don't need information from South America.

I remember her sweet, precise, scalpel-like voice. I don't need information from South America.

When Nick kissed me, I almost asked what a kiss from South America tasted like. But it was an empty question. It was a fleeting question, on which I chose not to dwell.

I have seen my father a few times. I went to Abidjan to visit him and his family. We talked a little about my mother. Not much. Besides me, the two of them didn't actually have much in common. Not even memories. I don't think they had even missed each other. I went to visit him twice with tickets that Fernando bought for me and I stayed fifteen days each time. Daniel came here last year, on a business trip to the United States. We went out for a few beers.

It was nice to go out for a few beers with my father. I paid the bill. He didn't want to let me but I insisted and said that he was my guest and added, with a lack of originality that was possibly touching, that the next time we'd have dinner at a French restaurant and everything. From time to time we talk on the phone. From time to time I talk to Florence on the phone. The last time I could hear Norbert's vacuum cleaner on the other end of the line. I never heard anything else about Isabel.

I have a job at the Denver Public Library – but not as a security guard. I sold Fernando's 1985 Saab and bought a Saab fifteen years younger because I don't know anything about cars and at least Saab was a familiar name. I'm not the talkative type. But people no longer hear an accent when I speak.

Would I have done things differently, if it were up to me – if I'd had choices, if I'd had a card deck of lives and could have chosen one instead of another? I would have. Not everything. I'd have changed just one detail, only one, at the end of a scene that took place over two decades ago.

My version would be like this:

The highways are an adventure in December in this part of the world. Fernando was on the road for much more than the usual six hours between cities on Interstate 25. There was snow and ice on the road. He left behind Trinidad, former residence of Bat Masterson and, in those days, the world sex change capital thanks to the operations conducted by the famous Dr. Stanley Biber. He passed a sign saying WELCOME TO NEW MEXICO LAND OF ENCHANTMENT and saw in his rear-view mirror a sign saying WELCOME TO COLORFUL COLORADO, with the Sangre de Cristo Mountains to the west.

When he arrived in Albuquerque I was in my room dreaming pint-sized dreams, dreams that were the size of my life, that fit easily through the bars of the crib. He and my mother embraced with the force of how deeply they missed one another. He went to bed with her. Later, after midnight, she made some soup and they sat in front of the Christmas tree to sip it.

It was supposed to be for good. And it was.

THANK YOU

to the University of New Mexico, especially Professor David Richard Jones, and to the University of Texas in Austin, especially Professor Sonia Roncador. For the home away from home and help with my work, I thank Leila Lehnen, Jeremy Lehnen, Malcolm McNee and Erô Silva. I would also like to thank Taís Morais, Cristina Brayner and Giulia Gurevitz. And my agents Nicole Witt and Jonah Straus.

Brazilian author **ADRIANA LISBOA** was born in Rio de Janeiro and currently resides in the United States. She has published eleven books, among which six novels, a collection of short stories and prose poetry, and books for children. Her work has been translated into English, French, Spanish, German, Italian, Swedish, Romanian and Serbian, and will shortly appear also in Arabic.

Among her honors are the José Saramago Prize for her novel *Symphony in White*, a Japan Foundation Fellowship for her novel *Hut of Fallen Persimmons*, a fellowship from the Brazilian National Library, and the Newcomer of the Year Award from the Brazilian section of IBBY (the International Board on Books for Young People) for her book of poetry for children, Língua de trapos (*A Tongue Made of Scraps*). In 2007, Hay Festival/Bogota World Book Capital selected her as one of the thirty-nine highest profile Latin American writers under the age of thirty-nine.

With degrees in Music and Literature, Adriana Lisboa performed as a Brazilian Jazz singer while living in France, and subsequently worked as a music teacher in Rio. She also translated into Portuguese such authors as Cormac McCarthy, Margaret Atwood, Jonathan Safran Foer, and Maurice Blanchot.

A NOTE ON THE TYPE

The text of this book is set in Bembo. This type was first used in 1495 by the Venetian printer Aldus Manutius for Cardinal Bembo's *De Aetna*, and was cut for Manutius by Francesco Griffo. It was one of the types used by Claude Garamond (1480–1561) as a model for his Romain de L'Université, and so it was the forerunner of what became standard European type for the following two centuries. Its modern form follows the original types and was designed for Monotype in 1929.